I SAW THE GHOST AND IT WAS WORSE THAN THE WORST HORROR MOVIE!

It was this man, or thing. His head rested on his right hip. He was holding it cupped under a leg which came out of his right armpit. His left arm was sticking straight out of his neck. He was standing on the other arm and his other leg. Otherwise everything else was okay. He was dressed in a costume.

"Boo!" he shouted and giggled.

"You're a ghost!" I said.

"None other. Gave you a scare, didn't I? Well, goodness gracious, I can't be expected to do everything. It was hard enough to materialize. Ever try it when the wind's blowing in the wrong direction?"

"I beg your pardon?" I said.

"Oh, dear me," he said, looking up and around at himself. "It took all that time, and I did it wrong."

"Boy, I'll say," I said. "First of all, can you put your head back on your neck? That would help."

Ghost In My Soup

Judi Miller

A BANTAM SKYLARK BOOK®
TORONTO · NEW YORK · LONDON · SYDNEY · AUCKLAND

RL 3, 008–012

GHOST IN MY SOUP

A Bantam Book / August 1985

Skylark Books is a registered trademark of Bantam Books, Inc.
Registered in U.S. Patent and Trademark Office and elsewhere.

ISBN 0-553-15310-2

Published simultaneously in the United States and Canada

PRINTED IN THE UNITED STATES OF AMERICA

O   0 9 8 7 6

For my godson, Bryan Weinstein,
with a special thanks to the original
Tracy and Scott Laidman

1

Blood Brothers

"Ouch!"

I wiped off my penknife and handed it to Ralphie.

"Now me," I said, closing my eyes. I felt the nick. My finger was spurting red blood. "Okay, you suck the blood from my finger, and I suck it from yours. That's how it's done."

"Are you sure?" Ralphie asked.

"Will you c'mon before it hardens. Yes, I'm sure. I saw it on TV."

"How come we didn't smoke peace pipes to become blood brothers?"

"Ugh. Who wants to inhale all that smelly smoke. Hurry up."

"Okay. Here goes. I'm going to suck your blood. Moooo—ha-ha."

When it was my turn, I had a hard time getting hold of his waving finger. "Ralphie, c'mon, or it won't take." I was more afraid of what disease I could catch from Ralphie's dirty finger than of tasting a little blood. Once he went without a bath or

1

shower for a whole week until his mother finally made him wash. The smell became too much for the family to live with. But Ralphie McLaughlin was a great guy. He was my best friend. Though I also played with Spider Schwartz and Mark Harris, it was Ralphie I liked best.

That's why the whole thing was so unfair. I had to move. How could I ever find another friend like Ralphie?

Just then he fell to the ground, rolled around, and kicked his feet. "The poisonous finger," Ralphie moaned. He kicked both his legs straight up in the air once, twice, three times. Then he lowered them slowly to the ground and lay still.

The sound of a horn honking made me jump.

Next came the unmistakable voice of my mother. "Scott, where are you? Time to go. Finish your goodbyes."

"Look, Ralphie," I said. "You're not dead."

He said nothing. He just lay there staring up at the sky with huge, unblinking eyes.

"Ralphie, we're leaving. Get up." I kicked him. He started to roll over, but then plopped back.

The horn honked again.

"C'mon, Ralphie. We're blood brothers now. That means we'll always be best friends."

Nothing. I couldn't even see him breathing. Gosh, he was a real pro! I didn't know anyone who could look up at a late August sky, when the sun was blazing, and not even blink their eyes.

"I *really* have to go now, Ralphie." There were

five quick honks right in a row. But he didn't move.

Shrugging, I turned to go. I had just gone around the side of his house to the front street, when I felt the wind being knocked out of me. I fell on the grass, and we wrestled for about a minute. Then I untangled myself from Ralphie and stood up. "I guess I really have to go," I said at last.

He nodded.

We just stood there. I stuck out my hand. We stared at each other. Then he took my hand and shook it. We gave each other a big hug, but just for a second. I didn't cry. What's to cry about? Just because he's been my best friend for as long as I can remember? Just because we've lived next door to each other all our lives? Just because I'm moving far enough away to still be close, but way too far away to see each other every day? I'm ten years old. Nothing can make me cry.

I waved to him a few times as I walked. "I'll call you later," I yelled. He saluted army fashion, clicked his heels, turned about-face, and walked away.

I could see the moving van in full view. It looked like a house on wheels. Right behind it was our car. In the car were my mom and dad, my dog, and my bratty little brother, Brad.

My dad punched the horn again and yelled, "Hurry up, Scottie, or we'll have to leave you behind." I wished they would.

When I got in the car, my mom said, "What's wrong with your finger? Did you cut yourself on something?" I looked down. There was a red stripe on my finger, but it wasn't dripping in puddles or anything.

"Yeah, I cut myself," I replied. I always believe in telling the truth. "But it doesn't hurt."

She handed me a tissue to tie around it. "Sorry I forgot the Band-Aids."

My mother's purse reminds me of a suitcase. We should submit it to the *Guinness Book of World Records*. To make up for not having Band-Aids, my mom took a banana out of her bag and handed it back to me. I wasn't hungry so I passed it to Brad, and just to be cruel, I didn't peel it. He sat there sucking on it happily. He may have just turned three but he was sure dumb. On the left was my dog, Prince II. He's a mutt, but you'd never know it.

Suddenly I saw Ralphie with a group of boys I hung out with. They were all waving. I shot up and sat backward, knees against the back seat. I waved like crazy until we turned a corner. Then they were gone. I sat down face-front with a plop. Brad looked up at me and giggled. There were times when I just wanted to smack that kid. I gulped. It felt as though a basketball was in my throat. I had to swallow a lot to keep it down. But I didn't cry or anything like that.

I couldn't believe that only a month had passed since my mom and dad told me the "wonderful" news. "Scottie," they said, "guess what? We're moving!"

Moving? Down the block? Around the corner near Spider? Oh, no. My dad had done so well in real estate that we were moving out of Mayfield Heights, and the house I was practically born in, to someplace really special. Chagrin Falls. My dad said, "You can probably have your own pony, Scottie. We have a stable." Big deal. Horses just stand there stomping and snorting and waving their tails.

Finally I told them the truth. "I'm not going."

I was really nice about it, and I promised to call and to send them a Christmas card. It's unfair to take a kid out of a place where he's perfectly happy and put him in a new place just so his parents can have a fancy showoffy house. I figured I could probably live with Ralphie until I graduated from high school. But his mother said Ralphie was one too many little boys as it is.

My parents kept on telling me what a great place Chagrin Falls was. Just about one of the nicest places to live in Ohio. We would be living in a house that was one hundred years old. I would have my own room that was nowhere near Brad's, who has a habit of singing in his sleep. I would make lots of new friends.

We continued to follow the huge moving van. Brad sat in his car seat, with his two chubby legs sticking out. My mom had finally opened his banana, and he looked as though he was foaming at the mouth. Everything about that kid bothered me. Especially his new habit, which was repeating whatever I said.

"All we have to do is unload the furniture," my

mom said. "The house is all decorated." She was really excited. "Nino is already there."

I met Nino once. He has a long mustache that curls at one end, black curly hair, and wears a black beret. I thought he was weird, but my parents said he was one of the best interior decorators in the city of Cleveland and its suburbs.

"And Scottie, you'll just *love* your room," my mom went on. "It's a *dream* room for a boy."

"Did Nino do that?"

"No, Daddy and I fixed it for you." Then she took hold of my father's hand, and they started that mushy stuff—looking at each other and stealing little kisses. I thought it was dangerous to drive with only one hand. Besides, they should be doing that sort of thing in private.

"Oh, this is my *dream* house," Mom squealed.

"Jack and Jill went up the hill . . ." Dad sang, and they both laughed. Now things were really getting corny. See, my dad's name is Jack and my mom's name is Jill. They thought this house was an improvement for them. It was a definite step down for me.

We passed the sign that said Mayfield Heights and went into Chagrin Falls soon after. You really couldn't make the trip on a bicycle. You could do it, but only if you packed a lunch. I saw the difference between the old neighborhood and Chagrin Falls right away. The houses were big and old. I'd heard Chagrin Falls was there before Cleveland, Ohio,

was. They had a lot of historical buildings and antique shops. My mother loves that.

Then we came to our house.

"This is it?" I said. If there was disappointment
in my voice, I guess I meant it to be there.

My mother was getting out of the car, dragging
her bag and Brad. "Oh, Skeeter, you'll like it, I
promise."

I got out of the car and looked up. And up and
up and up. It wasn't one of those neat little houses
everyone had in Mayfield Heights. All the houses
looked alike on our street. In fact, once Ralphie's
grandfather took a walk, came back, and went into
the wrong house. He just sat down and turned on
the TV. It was about twenty minutes before it struck
him that the furniture was different. But this house. It
was unique.

"It looks like a big old barn!" I shouted.

"It's one hundred years old!" my dad an-
nounced. I think he had already told me that about a
hundred times, too.

"What a great report for your history class,
Scootch," Mom said, trying to rumple my hair. I
ducked. In Mayfield Heights it would have rated an
A, but not around Chagrin Falls. Everyone's house
was probably one hundred years old.

"There's Nino!" my mom shouted. At that,
Prince II ran behind me and disappeared into the
woods that surrounded the sides and the back of the
house.

Nino was standing on the porch waving a red hankie. He had little bits of material safety-pinned to his shirt.

The moving van had started to unload, and I watched for awhile.

"Look around!" my dad said. I went to the basement, where my mom was unpacking. That's where her office was to be. She entered contests as a part-time job. So far she'd won two sets of luggage, a weekend in Niagara Falls for two, and one hundred and thirty-five jars of peanut butter. The creamy kind. I like the chunky kind, but my mother said we had to use it up. This practically ruined my life until I discovered I could put peanuts in it. And this publishing company had asked her to write a book called *How to Enter Contests and Win*. Actually I didn't think she was such a good example. She never won a lot of money or anything like that.

I walked up the steps from the basement and looked around the house. It had three floors, not counting the basement. They all had high ceilings. On the first floor was the living room, the family room, the dining room, my father's study, and in the center off the dining room was this really humongous kitchen. It was all set up with big copper pots and pans. On the second floor was my parents' bedroom, a guest bedroom, another guest bedroom, and Brad's room. Brad had to have both a crib and a little bed in his room. He had his good nights and his bad nights.

On the top floor, or what could have been an

attic once, was my room. I had to admit that it was really something. It had a sloped ceiling with wooden beams, brick walls, and a shiny floor with little rugs. I even had my own bathroom. There was a desk and bookcases and a pinball machine that worked without putting money in it. There was also a horse from a merry-go-round. Just for decoration. And the colors in the room were brown, beige, and rust. I just stood there. Yeah, a guy could really like a room like that. Only trouble was they put it in the wrong house.

When I got downstairs my mom stopped me. Her eyes were all bright and shiny. "Do you like your room, Scottie-pie? I really worked so hard on it."

I could see how excited she wanted me to be so I said, "Yeah, Mom, thanks. It's a swell room." But I didn't say what I really felt. What was the use of a great room if you were unhappy?

I went outside and into the yard to check over my bicycle. It was in good condition so I took off to look for someone I could play with. It seemed as if I was always pedaling uphill. The houses sure weren't next door to each other. Heck, Ralphie and I once fixed up walkie-talkies through our windows.

Finally I found a big yellow house with bright pink and white flowers all over the front yard. I parked my bike and rang the doorbell.

An old lady answered. "Hi," I said in my friend-liest new-neighbor voice. "Do you have any children. Er, grandchildren?"

"No, I'm sorry we don't," she said, smiling.

"But if you're selling magazines or candy, we'll buy them from you."

I saw another smile over her shoulder. "Who is it, Ellie?" A man, also with white hair, had come up behind her.

"What's your name?" she asked.

"Scott Sheldon," I mumbled.

"It's Scott Sheldon," she shouted to the man who was standing one inch away practically. "And you're . . .?" She waited.

"I'm just looking for someone to play with. See, we just moved in."

"Oh, dear, there are no children around here. Why don't you come in and have a nice cold glass of lemonade?"

"Gee, thanks," I said. "But I'm in kind of a hurry."

She nodded. "Well, try the other direction. I know I've seen children around somewhere."

I got back on my bike. It seemed so hopeless that I just went home. Home? My home was the old house in Mayfield Heights and always would be. I called Ralphie as soon as I got in.

"Hi, Mrs. McLaughlin. Can I talk to Ralphie?"

"Scott! How do you like your big new house?"

"It's okay. Is Ralphie there?"

"I'll tell him you called. He and Spider and Mark went on a bike picnic. I don't expect him back until dinner."

"Okay." I gulped.

Boy, they sure didn't waste any time having fun

without me. My mother and Nino were running around the house with the moving men to tell them where to put the furniture. My dad was banging something with a hammer. Brad had crawled inside a big cardboard box and was singing. I ran all the way up the stairs to my room.

Prince II was standing in the middle of the room as if he was waiting for me. That dog is unbelievable. I never showed him where my room was. He looked glum.

"Guess you don't like it much, either, do you, boy?" I said, patting him on the head. He moaned.

I looked out the window. I was closer to the sky than most people, and I looked up. I guess I wanted answers. I only knew that for the first ten years of my life I was happy. And now, for the first time in my life, I felt so unhappy I didn't know what to do. All because we moved. Finally I decided to crawl under my bed and cry. But just for a little while.

2

Tracy Troublemaker

I was pouring blueberries into my Cheerios. Food was about the only thing that was keeping me going. It got me through the last two days of pouring rain. But today the rain had definitely cleared. Maybe Ralphie could come over.

My mom came into the kitchen and plucked one of my blueberries. "Surprise," she sang. I looked up. A remark like that from a mother like mine could mean anything.

"Someone is coming over. Someone you can play with."

"No kidding!" I said. Finally some kids. "Gee, that's great, Mom," I said.

I was wondering if he had a bike. Maybe we could play some two-hand touch in the yard if it wasn't too wet. "Mrs. Deevers is a neighbor. And she's in charge of welcoming new people into the community. I think her daughter's name is Tracy."

"A girl?" My voice was about an octave higher than usual.

"Now don't act like that, Scott. You're a big boy

12

now. Who knows? You may even like her. It's nice to be friends with everyone."

A girl? Never.

"Sure, Mom, I'll play with her," I said and dumped my blueberry and Cheerios mess into a Hefty bag. Prince II finished it. He still had milk dripping off his ear when he went to my room.

Girls. I'd heard there were some that played football. But if she was anything like the girls in my old fourth-grade class, it was going to be awful. They were always silly and telling stupid jokes no one laughed at. Girls always stuck together in little groups, too.

My favorite spot in my room is on my bed, sitting on my knees and looking out the small window over the roof to the treetops. I could see our duckless duck pond and the little building that would eventually have horses. Then I saw a car pull up the driveway. A woman got out. And this girl jumped out from the other side. They passed under the front of the house, and I couldn't get a real close look at her. I didn't have to wait long, though.

"Scottie, company!" my mom practically sang up the steps.

As I walked out of my room I thought of my friends back home, Ralphie, Spider, and Mark. For almost a week I hadn't seen a living person under the age of twelve—except for Brad. Why did it have to be a girl?

The blueberries and milk in my stomach were fighting with each other as I walked downstairs.

Maybe it won't be so bad, I told myself. Maybe she likes sports. Maybe she doesn't giggle. Maybe my mother is right.

When I got down to the third to last step, I saw her standing there. I looked into her eyes and knew my troubles were just beginning. She had blond hair that hung over her shoulders in thick braids with ribbons. Her shoes were white—not dirty, played-in white but polished white. She had on one of those stupid play outfits that was pink-and-blue checks, and she wore a white blouse. Her socks were white, too, with a little rim of lace around the cuffs. *She'd* never play football!

But it was her eyes that got me. I couldn't take my eyes off them. They were large and round and very angry. I knew instantly that her mother had probably dragged her over to play with me. And that she didn't want to play with me anymore than I wanted to play with her.

Prince II rumbled. He's a very sensitive dog. Either that or he ate a bad blueberry. Mrs. Deevers got all excited over Brad. Everyone did. It wasn't that I expected her to get excited over how cute I was. It's just that, personally, I thought Brad was a fraud. In about ten minutes he'd walk up to her purse and dump it on the floor. Then she wouldn't think he was so adorable. She'd want to smack him.

"Want to see my room?" I asked Tracy.

"Okay," she said. I went up first, with Tracy following and Prince II trailing. Brad followed my mom and Mrs. Deevers. I heard my mom say, "Isn't it great to see the kids playing together so nicely?"

Tracy was the first kid to ever see my new room. "Here it is!" I said, throwing my arms out. She sat down on the bed and folded her arms across her chest. I waited. I felt stupid for saying that. After about a minute, she said, "Nice. My room is on the second floor."

"I have a pinball machine." She didn't say anything. Then I said in my British actor's voice, "Do you live nearby?"

"Yes, about five miles away."

Prince II groaned. That animal is uncanny. Sometimes I think he understands what everyone says.

"I have a dog, too," Tracy said. "Her name is Mitzi, and she's a French poodle."

"You should have brought your dog. I mean, there's a nice big yard."

"We have seven acres on our property. Besides, she gets carsick."

There was another long pause.

"What grade are you in?" I asked.

"Fifth," she replied. It came out as though she thought the question was stupid.

"Hey!" I said, pretending to be enthusiastic. "We'll be in the same class."

"Maybe not." She smiled. "In the fifth grade in my school you get divided up. You'll either get Mrs. Simon or Mr. Macri." She thought about it. "But we might have music or science together."

"What's *your* school like?" I asked, thinking she

probably said *my* street, *my* sidewalk, *my* everything. I mean, I was going to *her* school.

"It's okay," she said.

More silence. I cleared my throat. Tracy didn't even blink. Prince II watched us both, waiting.

Finally I swallowed and asked, "Wanna play a game?"

"Okay," she said.

I studied my shelves for something a girl would like. Then I turned around. "What about Clue?" I asked.

"Okay."

I turned back to get it but it wasn't there. It wasn't anywhere. But it had been there before or I wouldn't have asked.

"Clue, Clue," I sang to myself.

"What's wrong?" she asked.

"It's not here." I started to take my games out and stack them one by one on top of each other. I could see her eyeballs rolling toward the ceiling impatiently.

"Listen," I said, giving up on that game. "Maybe it got lost when we moved. What about Scrabble? Ever play that? I *know* it's here. I just saw it."

"I've played that before. I'm a really good speller."

I went back to get the game. But it wasn't there! I looked again. Then I looked all around. It was just there! I began to feel dizzy and frightened all at once. What was happening? I pulled out all my games and threw them on the floor. But it still wasn't there. I knew she must have thought I was crazy. I was beginning to wonder, myself, if I wasn't losing my marbles.

"Marbles," I mumbled.

"I don't want to play marbles. Why can't we play the games you said?"

She jumped off my bed. Prince II jumped, too, and started licking her hand, and she stepped away. Now that made me mad. He was only trying to be nice.

"Brad!" I said loudly. He must have been in my room.

"What? Who's a brat?" She was getting angry.

"Brad, Brad," I said. "My little brother must have gotten into my room. We'll find something else to play with."

"I don't suppose you have any Barbies, do you?"

"Any *what*?"

"Barbie dolls. You know."

"I don't play with dolls!"

"Well, I didn't expect *you* did. I just thought you might have a sister or a cousin who had some here."

"I'm not going to play dolls with *you*!" I almost screamed.

"Forget it," she said coolly. "I just asked. I expected to play alone. I needed something to do while you play with your boxes."

That did it. "Listen, I don't play with dolls, and I *don't* play with girls. I promised my mother I would be nice to you even though you're a girl. And this is what happens!"

"I promised *my* mother I would play with a boy because you're new to the neighborhood!"

I turned my back on her and started to look for my games. If we could play something, maybe it would be better. This was a disaster! But before I could find something else, Tracy went downstairs.

Feeling exhausted I went over to my bed, where she had left a little dent, and climbed up on it. Prince II climbed up with me. We looked out the window. It had started to rain again. I knew I should have followed her downstairs but I just didn't care.

It wasn't long before I heard footsteps on the stairs. I didn't turn around.

"Scott, you're being rude to your guest. Now, what's the problem?" Then I turned around. I saw she had her hands on her hips. I was in trouble. She was going to act like a mother now.

"Nothing," I said, shrugging. "Tracy doesn't want to stay up here and play."

"That's not what she said. She said you didn't want to play with her."

"What!" I was trying not to get angry. I knew that would just make things worse. "But the games we wanted to play were here. And then they weren't here. And *I* didn't take them!"

"Which games were missing?"

"Clue and Scrabble."

My mom went over to the shelves. She looked through the boxes I had put back. I looked at Prince

II. His ears had shot up. Like he'd seen something. He started to bark, and I had to get him to be quiet. Then my mouth dropped open. My mom handed me the two games.

"Here are the two games you were looking for, Scott," she said in a cold voice. It would have been better for me if she was still angry.

I just nodded. I couldn't believe it. Was I going crazy or was there something fishy going on?

I heard steps creaking and jumped. But it was only Mrs. Deevers and Tracy.

"Jill," Mrs. Deevers said, "I really should go. Tracy's getting restless. I wish school would start. You know, I was just on the way up the stairs when I found your little Brad had emptied my bag all over the floor." I almost started to laugh. She added, "He's so cute." But I don't think she meant it.

My mom followed them out and gave me a look that wasn't exactly friendly. Tracy stuck out her tongue at me when no one was looking. I said in my nicest voice, "See you at *our* school."

After they had left, my mom came back up to my room. "How could you do this, Scott. All I did was ask you to be nice to a girl. I should think you'd welcome having someone your own age around. But no, you have to play pranks."

"I didn't play any pranks, Mom."

"Scott Sheldon, don't get fresh with me. You and I are friends but I won't have you getting fresh."

I nodded. There was nothing else to do. How could I explain what happened? Maybe there were secret compartments in the walls. Maybe the games fell in. But that was impossible. Someone was playing a trick on me. Brad was the only other kid ever in my room. But Brad's not smart enough to play a trick like that. Prince II didn't do it. Something was awfully fishy.

Ralphie. I thought how he would react if Tracy were in the room. He would play pretzel. Ralphie was double-jointed. He could wrap his legs around his waist. Then he rolled across the room that way. Ralphie would never even be in the same room with Tracy. He hated girls. I missed him so much that I wanted to run all the way back to Mayfield Heights. Then I remembered. It was Monday. Ralphie had gone on vacation with his parents, and he would be back today.

I went downstairs to call him. There was no answer. They weren't home yet, probably. Besides, he would have called me—I'm his best friend. The more I thought about it, the more I wanted to tell him about the strange missing games. Ralphie would know who took them. I wouldn't tell him about trying to play with Tracy, though.

That night at dinner I tried not to say too much so I wouldn't get on anyone's nerves. My dad shot me a couple of sympathetic man-to-man glances, but I knew my mom was still angry. I guess Mrs. Deevers is some kind of important person to know in the neighborhood.

Sometime after dinner I went upstairs to play with my pinball machine. Then I read some *Mad* magazines and fell asleep. Not five minutes later, or so it seemed, I shot straight up in bed. Prince II started to howl, and I had to keep him quiet so I could hear the noise that woke me up. The noise sounded like iron chains clanking against the floor. My teeth were chattering as I got up out of bed.

"Who's there?" I said, like an idiot. I heard a low moan. I looked at Prince II. It wasn't coming from him.

I jumped back into bed and huddled under the covers, shivering. But it was quiet. It took me a long time to fall asleep. I wondered if that spooky sound had anything to do with the missing games.

The next morning the very first thing I did was to ask my parents if they'd heard the noise. They said they hadn't heard it and that I must have been dreaming. It just didn't seem like a dream to me. I figured, though, it had to be. But if I was dreaming, it was with a sound track.

3
Disappearing Acts

Later that morning my mom sat me down at the kitchen table for one of our "talks."

"I want you to be happy, Skeeter. What's wrong?"

As if she didn't know. "I miss my old friends," I answered.

"But you'll make *new* friends," she said as if it were easy. "It just seems bad now. You know what you're going through? A transition period. Just bide your time until school starts. Have you walked around all of our property yet?" She looked out the window and pointed—"We own all the way to the end of the woods. And look at that garden, Scottie. We're going to pull out all the weeds next year and plant new seeds." My mom has a husky voice that sometimes squeaks. She sounds like a television actress.

"Try?" she asked.

"Try," I agreed.

She took my hand and we shook.

I went outside and stood on the porch that looked over the property. The sun was out. I walked toward the woods. Suddenly I heard screaming. Turning around I saw my mother streak out of the house like lightning.

"Brad's missing!" she shouted. "I looked everywhere. He's not in the house. It's impossible for him to get out. The front door is kept locked, and he can't open the side door. Did you leave the front door unlocked? I told you not to!"

"Mom! Maybe he's in the basement. You know how he likes to rip your envelopes. Or maybe he's hiding under a bed." In a way I felt sorry for him. In Mayfield Heights he could go outside on the sidewalk as long as he didn't go in the street. Here, he was locked inside like a prisoner. Prince II had more freedom.

First we went to the stables. He had been saying, "horsey, horsey," for the last few days. My mom yelled, "Brad! Bradley!"

Then we looked in the tall weeds in the garden. Nothing but weeds. We walked back toward the stable. I jumped when my mom screamed. There was Brad standing up to his waist in the duck pond, which was filled with mud and green slime. He wasn't even crying or trying to get out. He just looked surprised.

"Brad!" Mom screeched. "Stay where you are."

He looked up then and almost lost his footing. He couldn't have drowned, I don't think, but my mom splashed in like a rescue squad. When she picked him up and covered him with kisses and hugs, he covered her with gook.

"How did you get out?" she asked him as if he could tell her. Brad is slow. He was three a few months ago and hardly talks. His eyes looked huge, and he wasn't blinking.

"Scott, you must have left the door open," Mom said, scolding *me*.

"But, Mom, I came out the side door."

"You think you did. You walk around with your head in the clouds sometimes."

Now that made me mad. Especially coming from my mother. I started daydreaming about how nice it would be if Brad really had disappeared. Then I could be the only child in the family again.

"But, actually, I guess it was my fault," my mom said. "He's bored. And he's so bright for his age. I'll just have to put him in a nursery school this fall."

Bright for his age. He can't even talk! He just imitates me.

In the kitchen she fixed us some milk and cookies after she had dunked Brad, shirt and shorts and all, into the tub. I looked at him closely. His eyes were still open too wide, and his hands shook a little.

"Here, Brad," I said, watching my mom glow, which she did everytime I treated him like something better than an animal. "Have another cookie."

". . . another cookie," he repeated and smiled up at me.

We all went down to the office in the basement.

Brad sat on the floor with his legs out and shredded newspapers. I helped my mom sponge and put stamps on all the envelopes she had addressed.

The phone rang. There was a wall phone extension in the basement. She said, "For you." I ran up the steps to take it in the kitchen.

"Space Invaders!" came the scream.

"Hiya, Ralphie," I said. "How was your trip?"

"Oh, we never went."

I felt a sinking in the pit of my stomach. I thought, Well, you could have called. But I didn't dare say anything. I was too embarrassed.

"How ya doing?" he asked.

"Nobody to play with."

"Same here. This morning Spider left for his grandma's, and Mark is on a plane to New York City. He said he's going to fly off the Empire State Building. With water wings. But how are we going to check? What if it's not in the papers?"

"Hey, Ralphie. Can you come over? For a day or something. It's really a great old house," I lied. "And there's a duck pond and a stable."

I waited while he went to ask his mother. He came back. "My mom said her car's still being fixed. Maybe your mom could pick me up."

I ran down the stairs and pleaded with my mom. "Not for the next day or so, Skootch," she said. "Don't forget we have to buy new school clothes, and you have an appointment with the dentist . . ."

I left her in midsentence and ran upstairs to Ralphie.

"She said, 'no,' too."

"Well, we'll get together," Ralphie promised.

After I hung up, I felt frustrated and sad again. I took the dish towel off the corn bread my mom had baked and sliced off a small piece. I didn't think she'd mind. There was still plenty. Then I put butter on it and let it melt. That and a glass of cold milk made me feel a little better. I covered the corn bread.

I went up to my room and then came back down for a carrot ten minutes later.

"Where's my knife?" my mom said.

"Huh?"

"My good bread knife. It sits right *here*." She was pointing to the big wooden knife-holder on the counter. It was kept way back so Brad couldn't reach it.

"Gee, Mom, I dunno," I said, innocently standing by a kitchen chair. "Maybe it got lost in the moving." I was really getting logical.

"No!" she snapped. "I had it last night."

"Maybe it's in the dishwasher."

". . . dishwasher," Brad repeated, smiling.

"You don't put that kind of knife in there. And this is a special one!"

That set my mom off into one of her bad moods. The kind when she really goes bananas and we aren't friends. Sometimes being ten isn't easy. She takes out all her anger on me. Then I'm supposed to be a smiling kid later.

"Scott Sheldon, how could you?"

"How could I what?" I said.

"You ate half of the corn bread I made for dinner. Besides the fact that we won't have enough, it's rude and inconsiderate. Just because you're unhappy. It takes a long time to make that recipe. I could probably go into the catering business and serve . . ."

I had to stop my mom then. It was either that or go under.

"Mom, I only had a small piece."

"Now you're getting fresh again." She brought the pan to the table. Half of it was gone. But I just took a small chunk! I knew I didn't take that much. I looked at Brad.

He looked up at me adoringly from his pile of shredded napkin. No, it couldn't have been him. He would have taken fistfuls, and the corn bread had been cut with a knife. Something was really fishy around here! I remembered the games that had disappeared and reappeared. I felt the best thing I could do was make myself invisible too. Why was I always getting blamed for things I didn't do?

Angrily, I went out to the yard and got on my bike. This time I rode in the opposite direction. By some strange turn of fate I got lucky. I found some new friends. In a way.

They were playing football in a big field. I watched for awhile, and then one shouted, "Hey, you! Want to play?" I was all excited until I got on the field and someone said to me, "It's only because we're short one guy."

I said, "Hi. My name's Scott." No one said anything. They looked through me, not at me. I could hear from the guys that were yelling that the leader was Big Mikey. Another was Blake, another Joey, another Kevin. But it was hard to remember because I didn't really meet them. We played for about an hour or so and then they stopped.

I went right up to Big Mikey and said, "Hi, I'm Scott Sheldon. We're new here and . . ." But he didn't let me finish. He nodded and walked away. All of the guys got on their bikes and took off. No one invited me to go with them. I just watched them leave. Then I got on my bike and went home.

After I had washed up for dinner, my parents gave me the FBI treatment about where I had been.

"Out," I said, shrugging. "On my bike."

"I didn't mean to lose my temper with you, Scottie," Mom said. "If you're that hungry, ask first." She smiled at me. I knew my dad had gotten to her. "Being a mother is a thankless job," she added, smiling.

"What you need are some friends your own age," Dad said. He's at his office during the day, so he solves everything after we've got it all figured out.

"I have some friends," I said, trying to keep a piece of lettuce inside my mouth.

Everyone looked up. Even Brad.

"Yeah, I played football with the guys this afternoon," I said importantly. "They asked me to play." My dad smiled, and I looked away.

I went upstairs feeling lonelier than ever. There was nothing to do, so I went to bed early. I was doing a lot of that lately.

The next day I thought I'd find the game again. But as I got on my bike I heard some screaming coming from my room. Then an unmistakable voice yelled down from the window.

"You get up here this minute, Scott Franklin Sheldon."

I gulped. I was in trouble, and I didn't know why.

I ran up to my room and found my mom holding the lost knife. "Very funny!" she said. But I knew she wasn't about to laugh.

"I didn't . . ."

"Don't ever lie to me, Scott. A prank is a prank. I'm asking you now, did you or did you not put the knife in your toothbrush glass?"

In my toothbrush glass? Why did I put it there? But I didn't! Something very weird was going on.

My mom didn't wait for an answer. She just stomped out of the room. I hopped up on my bed, not even bothering to take off my tennis shoes. Prince II hopped up next to me. It was a nice sunny day, but I didn't feel like going out.

Nothing made sense anymore. I didn't let Brad loose by mistake. Or did I? And the games. Did Brad play a trick on me? Who ate the corn bread? And stole the knife? Maybe I walked in my sleep. Then there was that night I heard spooky noises. I sat up straight, suddenly figuring it out. My hands were trembling. Prince II was barking at nothing.

I remembered the Halloween party we had in Ralphie's basement last year. All of us had sat huddled together. We were under a huge, white sheet pitched like a tent over our heads. We had to keep our eyes shut. Then our Cub Scout leader read a spooky horror story. Of course no one believed the story, so it was impossible to scare us. Except me. I was terrified.

They passed around this slippery, wet eye and some slimy, stringy hair for us to touch. All the while a record was playing moany, groany sounds like the ecological records my mom has. The ones that just have the sound of waves splashing against rocks. I honestly thought I would be the first ten-year-old kid to have a heart attack.

Then the sheet came off and the lights came on and the music turned to this disco stuff. Personally I thought everyone looked a little pale in the light. But I might have been imagining things. Then we got to see the table of special effects. Big deal. The eye was just a plain, old peeled grape. The hair was nothing but cold, cooked spaghetti.

But that was then. This was no trick. How could I have been so stupid? Of course! There was a you-know-what in the house!

4

Blood-Clot Brothers

When I woke up the next morning, the first thing I thought about was the night before last. I knew now it hadn't been a dream. Then I remembered this was the day Ralphie was coming over. I leaped out of bed. His aunt Marla was driving him. Wow! I couldn't wait to tell him about the you-know-what.

I was so excited I could hardly eat breakfast. I waited in the living room, and at ten o'clock I saw a car pull up. I dashed down the steps and outside. The car door opened and Ralphie got out. He ran toward me. I ran toward him. Then we stopped.

"Gee, Ralphie. It's good to see you again."

I got a closer look at him. His hair was funny. It had been combed wet and parted on the side. It looked plastered to his head, like on Sundays when he went to Sunday school. I started to laugh. "Funnnny," I said, but he wasn't paying any attention to me. Ralphie's such a pro.

His neck bent all the way back as he looked at

31

the house. Up and up and up. Watching him you
would have thought it was a skyscraper.

"Wow, this is really big," he said with no emo-
tion in his voice. He had some trick planned. I just
knew it.

I looked up, too. Well, I had to agree it was a lot
bigger than our house in Mayfield Heights.

"Wow," he said again. "This is like a mansion.
This is bigger than the Mayfield Heights Library."

"Oh, c'mon, Ralphie, very funny. The library
isn't big. This is just a hundred-year-old stupid
house, that's all. It looks like a big barn."

Then I had to catch him because he almost fell
backward. My stomach did flip-flops. I didn't think
he was joking.

"C'mon in. See my room," I said, skipping
ahead of him.

"Hello, Mrs. Sheldon," he said in a toneless
voice when we got into the kitchen.

"Well, hello, Ralphie. I'm making something
special for lunch in honor of your visit." That would
have been the day in our Mayfield Heights house
when she would have fixed us lunch. Things sure
changed.

Ralphie nodded stiffly.

He was quiet as he followed me up the stairs. I
kept hoping this was another act. I had read stories
of people from other planets who invaded earth and
stole the real people. They put zombies in their
place.

When we got up to my room, Ralphie just stood

there. Finally he said strangely, "Wow, this is really nice. A pinball machine and everything."

"Yeah, hey, let's play. You don't need any money."

"Your folks must have really struck it rich like my mom said."

"Nah," I said. "We just got this big old house because my dad's in real estate. My mom works, too, you know."

Ralphie didn't say anything. Prince II stood on two legs the way he always did with Ralphie. That way he was almost as tall as Ralphie was. But Ralphie was so busy looking around he didn't even shake hands with Prince II or scratch his stomach or wrestle. Finally Prince II got bored, came down, and rolled over moaning.

We played pinball for awhile. I beat Ralphie because I got to practice every night. Then we sat on my bed.

Finally I said, "Ralphie, I think there's a you-know-what in this house."

"What's a 'you-know-what'?"

"C'mon, you know what."

"What?"

I cupped my hands over my mouth and whispered loudly, "A . . . ghost! That's what."

"A what?"

"A *ghost,*" I said, trying not to shout. "Shh, he may be in this room right now."

"I don't believe in ghosts," he said.

I shot straight up. "You did! You said you did."

"Well, I still do. Maybe. But there wouldn't be any ghosts in this kind of house." He said it like a real know-it-all.

I stood up. "Why not? Things are disappearing. I'm getting blamed. Someone ate half a corn bread. And the bread knife ended up in my toothbrush glass." He giggled at that. Then he looked serious again. "And I had this . . . this guy over one day. We wanted to play a game, but every time I looked for one it was gone. Then my mom came up and the games were there."

"Thought you didn't have anyone to play with."

"I don't. It was my mother's friend . . . Terry. A real creep."

Ralphie nodded. "Still. I don't think ghosts can be in houses that are fixed up as fancy as this. I mean, if there are ghosts. Maybe they only exist in your imagination."

I rolled my eyeballs to the ceiling. My best friend. My very best friend in the whole world. That was the final blow.

"So what do you want to play?" I said quickly.

"I guess touch football. Why not call your friend?"

"Who? The ghost?"

He laughed. Which made it worse. He wasn't joking. "No, that kid, Terry. Is that his name?"

"Oh, him. No, he couldn't play. I told you. He's a creep. I think he plays with dolls."

Ralphie was leaning against the window with his arms behind his neck.

"Hey, let me see your finger," I said.

"Huh?"

"You remember that day when I moved. And we became blood brothers."

"Oh, here." He jabbed his finger in front of my face.

"It's smooth," I said. "So is mine. I wanted a scar."

He shrugged.

I took a deep breath. If you don't ask, how are you going to know. It wasn't that much time since he was my very best friend and next-door neighbor.

"Hey, Ralphie? You mad at me?"

He gave me a surprised look. "Nope."

I felt like an idiot. Maybe it would have been better just not to have said anything at all. But Ralphie had sure changed in a short time. Or else he was into something even I couldn't understand. He sure was a smart kid.

"Let's wait for the ghost," I whispered.

"How do you do that?"

"Well, all the other times I didn't do anything. He just showed up. Invisible though, if you know what I mean."

Ralphie didn't nod.

We sat there. The three of us. Ralphie was in the most comfortable spot on the bed, sitting up, his head against the pillow, with his legs straight out in front of him. His hands were behind his head, with his elbows sticking out like extra ears. I was sitting on the end of the bed. Prince II was perched on my desk chair, alert, his tongue hanging out.

I was keeping an eye on my games. I jumped up to check the box titles every once in awhile. Ralphie was eyeing the pinball machine. Prince II was facing the door.

After about fifteen minutes Ralphie said, "Maybe there's no ghost."

I threw my hands up in the air. "But how do you explain all those things."

Ralphie said, "I dunno."

"What do you mean you don't know? There has to be a reason for everything." There was no answer. "You don't think I'm lying, do you?"

Ralphie crossed his legs at the ankles. "I dunno."

I wondered again if the real Ralphie was in a rocket shooting to another planet and this Ralphie was an alien. How could it be as hard to talk to my best friend as it was to a stupid girl? Maybe *I* had been replaced by an alien in the night. Maybe that was what all this was. I had been taken to another planet. Then were my parents real? Brad could have been switched in the pool. Although it was a pretty good duplicate.

I started to ask Ralphie about the aliens when my mom called from somewhere midway on the steps.

"Ralphie has a phone call," she yelled up.

Boy, he was a guest and he averaged just about as many phone calls as I did. We both ran down the steps.

Ralphie picked up the phone, said about six

yeahs, and then hung up. "She's coming for me in a few minutes."

"But you said you'd have lunch here!" I protested. My voice went sky-high and that embarrassed me.

"I know, but my aunt said she couldn't get a manicure. Her friend's not home, so she has to pick me up now."

"Aw, gee," was all I said. My mom silently removed one plate from the table.

I went outside with Ralphie to wait. We didn't say much. All we did was kick pebbles. I turned around and saw a small, curly blond head at the screen door. Brad wanted to come out. If he could open the door he would have. He just stayed with his nose pressed to the door watching us.

When Ralphie's aunt came, he jumped into the car and waved goodbye. His aunt Marla, who always wears bright red lipstick and sunglasses even when it's not sunny, said, "Wow, Ralphie has ritzy friends. Some house. Some neighborhood. You must love it here, Scottie."

"S'okay," I replied. I wasn't going to say I liked the old neighborhood better.

When Ralphie left, my mom, Brad, and I had hot dogs, potato salad, salad salad, and root beer for lunch. Brad dropped the hot dog out of his bun, and Prince II jumped for it. Served Brad right for not hanging onto things. Prince II sat under the table, and I patted him on the head.

"I'm sorry your visit didn't work out well," Mom

said. Then she added quickly, "I mean, that Ralphie had to leave so early."

"Mom? How old do I have to be to drive a car?"

"Sixteen, dear. We'll teach you when you get your driver's permit."

Sixteen. What good would that do? I would have to wait six years to get back to Mayfield Heights. With nothing else to do I took my bike and went out to find those guys again. I found them.

That night at dinner, my dad said, "Well, Scottie, tell us about your day."

Everyone looked up at me. Even Brad, who was sitting in his high-chair. I was beginning to feel funny. "Ralphie came over," I said, smiling, reaching for another chicken leg.

Everyone smiled and nodded. They seemed to be waiting. I said, "We had fun."

I went to bed early that night, and I got up early. About three o'clock in the morning. I was right in the middle of this weird dream. Tracy's braids were seven feet long. She was out cold. I wrapped her in her braids and stashed her in the freezer. Someone was chasing me. There were deep moans. I thought it was coming from Tracy, because her vocal chords would be frozen. Then I woke up. My blanket was on the floor, my pajamas were sticking to me, and I was twisted up in the sheets.

I knew I was awake. Prince II leaped onto the bed. Just for good measure I pinched myself. It hurt.

And those moans I thought I had heard in my sleep were getting louder and louder. . . .

5

Night of the Living Ghost

The moans stopped for a minute. Then I heard real chains clanking. Clunkety-clunk, getting closer and closer. Then the moans again, worse than a pack of dogs howling together. I moaned a little myself as I edged closer to the window. Which wouldn't do me any good unless I could unhinge the screen fast and leap. Prince II had jumped on my bed, but he was no help. He was sitting hunched over, quivering. His paws were over his eyes. Terrific—he was supposed to be a watch dog! Suddenly I started to panic. Maybe he could see something I couldn't!

Like . . . a . . . ghost. I couldn't swallow, but when I did, I could hear it. The moaning, clinking sounds were moving closer, but I couldn't see anything. I stuffed my knuckle in my mouth. If I cried out I didn't want *it* to hear me.

Then all the sounds stopped. I felt blind, deaf, and unable to speak. Prince II was shaking so much I felt as if I was on a vibrating machine. I wanted to scream.

A few seconds later, the sounds started again.

Closer. Clearer. The sound of chains gliding across the wooden floor. A moan that was like someone being tortured. Maybe it was the Ghost of Christmas Past coming early? But to top it all off, the lamp at the end of my bed was glowing in the dark! It was shaped like a clown, and the eyes were staring right at me.

I just couldn't stand it. Sprawling across Prince II, I flicked the lamp on. Then I pulled my knees up to my chin to stop my teeth from chattering.

Just then I *knew* someone—or something—was in the room with me. It was the kind of feeling you get walking down a street on a dark, spooky night. You know someone's behind you but you don't turn around. I was even too scared to breathe.

I told myself—okay, what's the worst that can happen? Ghosts can't shoot you. They can't sink their teeth into your neck. They can't eat you. Maybe they could turn *you* into a ghost!

I screamed softly, but quickly clapped my hand over my mouth. It sure knew I was here now. I dove under the blanket with Prince II, holding on to him tightly. The two of us were shaking so hard the bed was dancing around.

Suddenly, I thought I heard a voice over the moans. Could ghosts really talk? Quaking, I listened harder. Yes, it was a word. But I must have heard wrong. I peeked out from under the blanket.

It had said, "Whoops."

As if on signal, Prince II started barking as though we were being robbed.

I looked around frantically. Where had that voice come from? The chains were clanking again. But it sounded as if they were being dropped with a thud and picked up again. Several times. The moaning had changed too. It sounded more like an apology. Maybe it isn't a ghost after all, I thought. Maybe Ralphie and the old gang had come over to play a trick on me. Maybe this was a horror movie. Maybe I had fallen into the wrong time machine or something. Maybe I was right about the alien planets taking over. Maybe I should get under the bed.

I dove under, and Prince II stayed on top. He was jumping up and down, and then he let out a long, loud howl. I peeked out from under and sucked in a gasp. A head went flying across the room! A real head. But it was transparent. A ghost's head! The head teetered back and forth on the chair in front of my desk. Then it smiled and settled. It had a bald dome with long hair falling like fringe on the sides. It wore a pair of old-fashioned spectacles. I suddenly felt sick. I mean, there was a head that traveled across the room. It wasn't flying on wires. And I knew those eyeballs were real. Not peeled grapes.

I felt a surge of bravery then. I crawled out from under the bed. I was once more the hero of my daydreams as I went looking for the right weapon to slay the transparent ghost—or was it ghost's head?—with no body? Maybe the body was attached to the head sitting on my desk chair but it was invisible! If so, how could it sit like that? My hands were trembling as I tried not to stare at the head. I stuck my hand in the top drawer of my night table. I located my pocket knife, two pennies, some dried leaves, my rubber-band ball which was two inches wide, and my slingshot. My slingshot! I put one of the pennies in, aimed nowhere, and fired at nothing. All that did was make me feel better. For a second.

Now the room was starting to turn colors. It was definitely getting a greenish-gold cast to it. Prince II began to look like a Day-Glo dog. I ducked further under the bed, peeking out under the overhanging sheet. Prince II was going bananas on top. I thought, foolishly, of screaming for help. Then my parents could come up and save me. But then they might be hurt. And who would help me later?

The light was spinning. I gasped. It was coming together and forming a cone. Like a greenish-gold tornado. Then I heard awful grunting and groaning. The same voice as before said, "Oh, dear me." I thought my eyes would pop out as the head flew backward across the room. Then an arm in a coat sleeve went by. Then more pathetic groaning. And finally an exasperated, "Oh, my, what a bother."

I tried to sit straight up. But I bumped my head on the bed, forgetting I was under it. Then I climbed onto the top of the bed, and Prince II crawled underneath. His tongue was hanging out almost to his chin, but he wasn't panting. Then I thought I'd pass out. I got very dizzy. My tongue felt fuzzy. I felt as though I was on a roller coaster going down.

I saw the ghost and it was worse than the worst horror movie!

It was this man, or thing. I couldn't see him, or it, that well. But who would want to? His head rested on his right hip. He was holding it cupped under a leg which came out of his right armpit. His left arm was sticking straight out of his neck. He was standing on his other arm and his other leg. Otherwise everything else was okay. I mean, all the parts looked okay. He was dressed in a costume. His chains were in a little puddle around him.

"Boo!" he shouted and giggled.

"You're a ghost!" I said, my teeth chattering like it was midwinter.

"None other. Gave you a scare, didn't I?"

For some reason that made me angry. I mean, who was he, or it, to say I was scared? If I was all that frightened I wouldn't be sitting there. I would have jumped out the window. What kind of ghost says "whoops," anyway.

Then I panicked. What if this was a trick and he would do something bad to me for not being scared.

Instead he said, "Well, goodness gracious, I can't be expected to do everything. It was hard enough to materialize. Ever try it when the wind's blowing in the wrong direction?"

"I beg your pardon?" I said, stuttering like I did when I was in second grade.

"Materialize. Make myself so you could see me," he said proudly.

"Uh-huh," I said. Maybe I was dreaming after all. No ghost I ever heard of looked like that. It would be hard enough to tell everyone there was a ghost.

But they'd never believe what he looked like.

"Oh, dear me," he said, looking up and around at himself. "It took all that time, and I did it wrong."

"Boy, I'll say," I said. "First of all, can you get your arm back on your shoulder? Can you put your head back on your neck? That would help."

There was a flash of greenish-gold light and he disappeared. But when he came back he had done it! I was amazed.

"Okay," I said. "You look much better. Now, what you need to do is put your right arm on your right shoulder. But first you'd better get your leg out and put it down on the floor with the other one."

Another display of bright lights. It took him a little longer this time. As I was waiting, I thought: Too bad no one will believe this. I bet I could make a million dollars! But I knew somehow no one would.

I could see the ghost again, and I started to laugh. Prince II just snarled.

I couldn't stop myself. I rolled on my bed and laughed some more. He had his legs all mixed up. The right one was on the left side and the left one was on the right side. The result was he was pigeon-toed and his knees said "hi" to each other. It was so funny. He went to all that trouble and left out one detail.

"Oh, dear me," he said after awhile. "Give me a second."

Then he scrunched up his face, grunted, the green lights flashed, and he vanished for one second more. He came back smiling. I stared. It was much easier to make out who and what he was. He was a fully clothed man who looked as if he had rented some clothes from one of those costume stores. I could see him, but because he was transparent, I could also make out the patterns on the curtains hanging on the window behind him.

"Who are you?" I asked, now a little in awe.

At the same time he asked, "I suppose you want to know who I am?"

We stared at each other. I was holding Prince II's jaw shut with my hands, which he almost bit off he was so excited.

"I," he said, with a grand gesture, "I . . . am . . . the . . . ghost . . . that haunts Mallory Manor."

"Oh! Is that across the street?" I asked. "Funny, but I sensed there was a ghost in this house, too."

He put his hand up like a stop sign to halt all my questions. "No!" I seemed to have made him angry. "*This* is Mallory Manor. I built it one hundred years ago. I am Malcolm Mallory. And I'm here to haunt you!"

I got scared again. As he leaned over, he picked up his swirl of chains, crossed his eyes, and swayed and moaned. He staggered toward me but tripped on all his chains. His head fell off and tumbled to the floor, and he had to stop to put it back on. I just couldn't help it. I started to laugh again.

So did he. Mr. Mallory didn't at all look like what I expected. He wasn't tall and he wasn't short. He wore a longish jacket and striped pants and a

ch on a chain. Then there was that
...l and shiny, and his dirty-white hair
...g on the sides. His spectacles were
...his nose, looking as though they would
...second. When Mr. Mallory laughed, his
belly ...ok like a plate of Jell-O. Then he took off his
specs and wiped them with the end of his jacket.

"Not much of a ghost, am I?" he asked.

I didn't know what to say.

"But then again," he went on, "what can you expect? I didn't ask for the job. Did anyone give me a lesson? Did anyone show me the ropes? No, sirree. When I was Martha's own special ghost I never had to scare anyone."

"Martha?"

"Yes, Martha, my wife. The late Mrs. Mallory."

"Gosh, I'm sorry to hear that. When did she pass away?" I said.

"In 1900. It was in the spring." I shook my head in disbelief. This couldn't be happening to me. Then I looked at the see-through man. It couldn't be? It sure was!

"I went in 1885. Just after we built this wonderful house. It was an untimely death, so I guess the powers that be decided I shouldn't rush off. I stayed with Martha, and she was the only one who could see me. Then I lived in the attic for awhile. Here," he said, gesturing. "Not for too long. Only eighty years." He hooked his thumbs in his vest, proud of himself. "Say, did you know that years and years ago, when children used to play here, it was called the Haunted House? They said there was a ghost in it. And there was. Me!" he laughed. "Oh, my. How I would moan and groan and clank my chains. I really scared them off. Of course, I was a lot younger then. I guess I didn't scare you much, though."

"You did. Really you did!" I insisted, but partly because I wanted to make him feel better. "Honest. And you really scared Prince the Second."

"Prince the Second, is it?" He bent down to pat my dog's head with his filmy hand, and Prince II snarled at him. Prince II wasn't himself. "What happened to Prince the First, if I may ask?"

"Run over by a car," I said. "My mom smoked a whole pack of cigarettes before she got up enough nerve to tell me."

He rubbed his chin. "Horseless carriages, you mean. Oh, yes, I've seen plenty of them. But a woman who smokes. I've never seen that."

"Oh, yes, a lot of them do. But my mom quit. For a while she sucked on lollipops, but she licked that habit, too. Hey, are you the one who's been playing all those tricks on us?"

He nodded. "My powers aren't what they used to be. Years ago . . . Well, years ago . . ." and his voice drifted off.

"Can anyone else see you, Mr. Mallory?" I asked.

"Only a select few. Specifically, Martha could. You can. And your baby brother can. None of the other people in this house or those you've brought in have the ability. They are not believers you see. Not even converts."

"Then only children can see you, huh? They usually believe in ghosts."

"Some don't. And some adults do. Some adults haven't crossed over, you know."

I nodded as if I understood. Then I said quickly, "Crossed over?"

"Crossed over. That's a grown-up who hasn't forgotten all the mysterious joys of childhood, who is eternally curious, delightfully trusting. My Martha was like that. It's a rare breed. Don't even trouble yourself looking for them. People of your generation tend to believe only what they see."

"Hey, I have an idea!" I said.

"What's that, my dear boy?"

"My name is Scott, Mr. Mallory. Why don't you call me that?"

"Scott," he said and added, "And you must call me, not Mr. Mallory, but Malcolm."

"My idea is that, instead of you trying to scare me, we can be friends. I sure need one right now, Malcolm. That way you don't have to knock yourself out trying to be the perfect ghost."

"Good thinking. We could have a lot of fun. And now, if you'll excuse me, I'm beginning to vibrate."

"Vibrate?"

"Yes, I told you. My powers are rusty. So pretty soon I'll fade and blow out like one of those electric bulbs. You know how they kind of sputter and go *poof.*" Then there was a little puff of smoke, and he vanished.

I crawled back into bed. It was still dark. My clock radio showed it was three-thirty in the morning. The dog was rumbling. I was never so wide awake in my life, but I fell asleep instantly, knowing that when I woke up I would know it hadn't been a dream.

6

Hostigazerious

The next morning when I came down to breakfast, my dad had already left. Brad had taken off all his clothes and was sitting and playing with the pots and pans he had taken out of the cupboards. My mom was drinking a cup of coffee and reading the paper. Malcolm was sitting on the kitchen counter, his legs swinging, his specs falling off his nose. Because he was transparent, it looked as if he was sitting *in the* kitchen counter. He reminded me of the pictures I'd seen of Benjamin Franklin.

"Hi, Malcolm," I said. Then I clapped my hand over my mouth.

"What's that, Skeeter?" Mom asked, not looking up from the morning paper.

I just said, "Hi, Mom."

"Hi, dear. What do you want for breakfast? What about cereal and some nice fresh bananas." She pointed to the clump of bananas. I watched Malcolm licking his fingers and saw the banana peel right beside him. Uh-oh.

"Oh, you already had one. Then just have the

cereal. But, Scott, dear, throw away the peel when you finish. That's what they invented garbage disposals for." Quickly I picked up the peel as if it were contaminated. Malcolm winked at me. Then my jaw dropped. I thought ghosts didn't eat. But the whole banana, now a chewed-up lump, sat in his stomach. It was as though I was looking at an X-ray.

"Mom," I said cautiously. "Do you see anything funny about that cabinet over the counter. Like it was built lopsided or something." Malcolm was sinking into it. You couldn't miss him. Or at least I couldn't.

Anything wrong with her dream house was enough to get her immediate attention.

She looked up sharply. And right through Malcolm. He smiled back at her. "Nope, it looks okay to me." Then she looked at me. "Anything wrong?"

"Wrong? What could be wrong?" Maybe she'd heard the noises and wanted to test me.

"I didn't sleep so good last night. There was a lot of noise."

"We didn't hear any noise. What kind? Was there a storm?" she asked.

"Oh, you know. Chains and clunking and moaning and that sort of stuff." Even as I said it, I wished I hadn't.

She smiled. "Oh, you were having nightmares again. But you are awfully *hostigazerious* this morning. I noticed it when you came down."

I don't know who invented that word. I was surprised to find out none of my friends in Mayfield

Heights knew what it meant. When they did, everyone used it. It means jittery and nervous and not yourself. My mom gets *hostigazerious* a lot, and when we remind her, she calms down. My eyes were glued to the door, where Malcolm was passing through to go outside. Then I remembered it was okay. Nobody could see him except Brad and me, and he wouldn't talk. But I thought of one thing that really got me *hostigazerious*.

No one could see the ghost except Brad and me. But objects Malcolm lifted would probably look as if they were flying through the air.

That night at dinner we had consommé. My mom is into gourmet cooking, and we're her guinea pigs. I looked into my soup and saw, as clear as in a mirror, Malcolm's reflection. I did a double take. I never knew ghosts had reflections. It was very clear. Clearer than he sometimes was.

Before I knew it, my plate of soup was being lifted by Malcolm. I guess he liked soup, too. But I had to stop it in midair. He was standing right behind me. Holding the plate. There was nothing for me to do but grab the plate and gulp down the hot soup. My dad stared at me. My mom said, "What good is a fancy house, if your kid's a slob." I don't think she was kidding, either.

I tried to give Malcolm a signal to stop fooling around. I made a face at him, but my back was to the table. When I turned around I found my mom and dad staring strangely at me.

"Have you been playing with your new friends, Scottie?" Dad asked.

I was eyeing Malcolm, who was standing on his head with his feet against the refrigerator, which is pretty good for a one-hundred-year-old ghost.

"Yeah," I said. Which was half true. I was trying to play with them, but they didn't want to have anything to do with me.

"Scott," Mom said. "Your father wants to have a talk with you." Gee, she sounded serious.

"I didn't do anything wrong."

". . . do anything wrong," Brad said, grinning.

"Who said you did anything wrong?" Dad said. "You'll be eleven soon, and your generation grows up much faster than mine. Everything goes faster than it did in my generation."

I looked from one to the other. They knew about Malcolm. But, that was impossible. They said they didn't believe in ghosts. They didn't even believe in horoscopes. Then it had to be the fact that all the guys on the field treated me as if I had BO. And they didn't even know my name. Yeah, that was it— one of my dad's pep talks. He had found out his kid was a loser.

I turned as red as the ketchup that slithered onto my yuchhy nongourmet liver and onions and said, "Sure, Dad, right after supper."

". . . right after supper," Brad said.

Meanwhile Malcolm was rocking in the white antique rocking chair. I guess it looked as though

there was a pretty strong breeze coming through the
open window, but it wasn't a windy evening. That
chair was rocking just a bit too much. I jumped up
and sat on the chair, right on top of him. I hoped I'd
been quick enough so everyone would think I was
doing the rocking. Boy, I bet I looked funny rocking
my head off for no reason at all.

My mom looked across the table at my dad
meaningfully.

"*Hostigazerious,*" she said.

"*Hostigazerious,*" he agreed.

Brad didn't say anything. Not that the word was
too much. He only echoes me.

When it was dark, my dad and I had our man-
to-man talk in the back yard. He wanted to go upstairs to my room, but there was no telling what
Malcolm would pull. Right before, when I was helping my mom clear the dishes, Malcolm was standing
in front of the sink, smiling at me. My mom passed
right through him. I held my breath!

"Scott!" Dad called.

I grabbed an old peanut-butter jar from the
kitchen. Then I poked holes in the top for air. It
wouldn't hurt to try and catch some fireflies while we
were out there. My mom kind of snuck upstairs, saying she had to put Brad to bed.

"Scott, hurry up."

Slapping a mosquito I sat down on the back
porch with my dad. "Someday we'll close this in and
build a patio right out there," he said. I nodded and

slapped another mosquito. Was that why he wanted to talk? About the house?

"This is hard for me, Scott. I didn't have such a close relationship with my dad. Different generation, you know."

I unscrewed the lid on my firefly jar and let it sit at my feet. "I know what you mean, Dad, I wanted to ask you but I thought you'd laugh." He did know about Malcolm.

"Laugh? No, Scottie. Every boy should know. I guess your generation needs to know a little earlier, that's all. Television. All that television."

He was right. I once saw these old reruns of *Topper*, where only this one man could see two ghosts who kept teasing him. Now I know how that man felt. But then Dad knew, too. "Just what exactly do you want to tell me, Scott. Listen, I know when I was your age I picked up a lot on the street."

"Were they transparent, like mine?"

He didn't say anything for a moment. Then he said, "I beg your pardon, Scottie?"

"Your ghosts. Could you see them? You see, I'm the only one that can see mine. At least, I think. Mom can't. But can you? I guess adults lose the knack. But when you were a kid . . ."

"Scottie, what on earth are you talking about?"

"Ghosts! Isn't that what our talk is about?"

"No, it is not. And you know what your mother and I said about all this ghost talk. You have a good imagination, Scottie. Believe me, that's good. But there are no ghosts, or goblins or witches. Not even at Halloween."

I felt a hopeless gloom. It was worse than the loneliness of having no friends.

He cleared his throat. "Actually I was talking about the facts of life."

"Sex? You wanted to talk about that?" I said. "Oh, don't worry about that, Dad. I know all about everything. We had that in school. Then I got books in the library. And you can see it on TV all the time."

"But surely you didn't get it all right. When I was your age I thought you could have babies by kissing. Gee, I feel terribly old-fashioned about this, Scott. Your mother kind of put me up to it. Because of the way you reacted to the little Deevers girl. She thought you might be developing certain feelings."

Tracy. The thought of her disgusted me. "Hey, Dad. I'm really not interested in girls. Just sports. I don't think I'll like girls for another ten years."

As I got up to go in, I could feel his hand clapping my back. I raced to the phone in the basement. I put my firefly jar, which was empty, on the kitchen table as I passed by.

Quickly, I dialed. After a few rings Ralphie answered. Was I glad he was home.

"Ralphie?"

"Yeah."

"It's me. Listen, your cousin Rob was wrong. You can't get babies by kissing."

"How do you know? It can happen sometimes."

"My dad told me you can't."

"You talked about s-e-x with your *dad!*"

"Yeah." Suddenly I felt self-conscious. Sometimes, lately, Ralphie sounded stupid. Maybe he wasn't as smart as I thought.

"Well, I'll check it out," he said.

"Sure, Ralphie. I'll see you." I put the phone down and felt an ache in my chest. I guess I really didn't care if he called me back about it. I knew I was right. Terrific. Some best friend. I climbed the three flights of stairs backward. Who was I kidding? Ralphie wasn't my best friend anymore. How could life change that fast?

I hated the house then. It had made me lose my friends. It put me out in the woods. And I had a nutty ghost who was nothing but trouble. And who I'd thought was going to be my friend.

When I got up to my room, I cupped my hand around my mouth and yelled. "Hey, Malcolm. Mr. Mallory. Where are you when I need you? You said we could be friends. Maybe we'd better talk about the kind of friend I meant. Because as it is, you're just about the only one I have."

Prince II jerked his head up, listening. I thought he saw or sensed something. Maybe Malcolm was preparing to materialize. I waited. I thought I heard a faint "Whoops," but I could have been imagining it.

Getting ready for bed, I thought, Boy, some friend Malcolm the Ghost turned out to be. With friends like that who needed enemies. Well, maybe I'd make new friends in school. My mom had gotten everything ready for me. I looked at the chair in front of my desk. Clean shirt and pants, my lunchbox, and some sharp pencils. I had tossed my favorite hat on top. The blue polished cotton with the silver wings.

Maybe tomorrow would be better. I was bound to make friends my first day at school.

7

Howard Fierman's Habit

The day after Labor Day was a beautiful day. The school bus let me off right on the corner. I figured if I pretended I didn't know her, the school bus would pull away and no one would see. But there was my mother holding Brad and waiting for me. His nose was all runny, and his fly was open. I think some of the kids did see her. I mean, she was jumping up and down yelling, "Skeeter, Skooter!" But I don't know if it really mattered.

"Hi, Mom," I said, casually.

"Scott Sheldon, you looked a million miles away then, like you didn't even see me."

"No, I saw you, Mom." Funny how parents who try so hard to understand their children just miss the boat sometimes. And worse, I couldn't say—"See, I was trying to ignore you. Because none of the other kids' mothers met them at the bus stop."

"So. Tell me everything. How was your first day at school?"

"It was okay."

"Did you meet all the kids?"

"Yeah."

"And?"

"They were okay."

"Did you get in Tracy Deevers's class?"

"Yeah." Big deal. It was awful.

"I'm so glad you like school," Mom said. "I knew once the school year started you'd be more like your old self again. C'mon, Skooter-pie, let's crunch the leaves on the ground."

You really can't get mad at my mom. There she was squishing the dry, brittle leaves, with Brad riding piggyback. She's kind of cute, I guess. And she acts like a little kid sometimes.

My mom and Brad went downstairs, and I trudged upstairs. I had some math problems to do. I knew from last year it was better to get them done early, and before my dad got home. My dad likes to help me with my homework and it takes twice as long. But he's starting to catch on to the new math.

I was just figuring out the last problem when something made me look up. A breeze fluttered the curtains and a leaf fell to the windowsill. In another second, I could see Malcolm sitting, though you could see through him, on my bed. He had his legs crossed and was smoking his pipe, which was also transparent.

He was smiling sheepishly.

"Well," I said. "Now's a fine time to turn up."

"I think you're cross with me, Scott."

"Yeah, I *am,*" I said. "You keep playing tricks.

Any minute now I'm going to get into trouble. If I don't cover up for you, I'm accused of pranks."

He smiled and scratched what was left of the white hair on his head. "Funny, now that I remember, a family by the name of Dominick lived here round about 1927. There was a lad about your age, and he needed a friend. We used to play that way, and he loved it. We had some pretty hair-raising experiences, too. Like the time we played catch with all the fruit in the fruit bowl, and his dear old grandma saw the bananas and apples and pears flying through the air." He chuckled.

"How did that kid handle it?"

"He suggested Grandma needed new specs." At this, Malcolm held his stomach and his belly jiggled around.

"Mr. Mallory, Malcolm," I began, clearing my throat. "I meant for us to be friends. Now, I don't mind a few pranks, but I meant a real friend. I have no one to play with here. But also no one I can really talk to. Tell my secrets to."

Malcolm sat up, alert. "Oh, yes, dear boy, tell me your secrets. It's been ages, really, since I've had a nice chat."

"Well, today was the first day in school and it was . . . awful."

"Dipped a little girl's pigtails in an inkwell, did you?"

I thought of Tracy's thick yellow braids and how she was always flicking the tips with her fingers and twirling them. "No, we don't have inkwells anymore. We have ball point pens now. Besides I don't sit behind Tracy. I sit behind Howard Fierman.

"Do you want the whole horrible story from beginning to end?" I asked.

"By all means, dear boy," Malcolm said and then sat on, or in, my desk.

"Well, the school bus picked me up. I was all set to be very friendly and try hard. First off, I heard this loud whisper, 'Here comes a new kid.' Someone stuck their foot out and tripped me. I almost fell flat on my face while the bus was rolling. What do you say after that?"

Malcolm shook his head and made clicking, sympathetic sounds with his tongue.

"I tell you, by lunch, I thought I was a deaf mute. None of the kids seemed to know I was there. And I wasn't going to bow down to Miss-High-and-Mighty Tracy Deevers just because I'd met her once."

Malcolm nodded.

"Then came lunch." I clapped my hand to my forehead. "And it was disgusting."

"Why?"

"Uh, well, see, I sat next to Howard Fierman in the school cafeteria. And I lost my appetite."

"My, my, that's a real tragedy," Malcolm said sympathetically. I was beginning to think our friendship would really work out.

"He was the only one who would sit next to me and be my friend."

"Well, that's nice."

"Nope, he's just about the most unpopular kid in the class. Know why?"

Malcolm shook his head.

"You'll never guess. I mean, he didn't do it while he was eating his bologna sandwich. . . . Are you sure you want to hear this?"

Malcolm nodded.

"He picks his nose and eats it."

"Disgusting!"

"I told you. How can I eat when he's sitting next to me?"

"I understand your point," said Malcolm. I was beginning to feel better about things and then I heard footsteps outside my door. In two seconds Malcolm completely vanished into thin air. I heard a faint "Whoops." He didn't have to do that, but it was too late. How long would it take him to materialize later? While I was shaking my head, my mom walked into the room. She looked around. Then she turned to me and said, "Oh, I thought you had a friend over."

I didn't say anything.

"Scott, I could have sworn I heard you talking to someone. Unless you're starting to talk to yourself." I thought I detected a look of sadness on her face then.

I just kept staring straight ahead. I figured that was my best bet. Then I spotted my radio and said, in a brilliant stroke, "Oh, yeah, I just turned off the radio. Talk show."

She smiled. "Oh, of course. Listen, Scotty-scoot, I hate to bother you but it doesn't look as though you have plans . . . I mean . . . that is to say, could you baby-sit Brad for just a few hours Saturday? I don't have a regular baby sitter yet and the ones I called said no, and, Scottie . . . I have an appointment I've just got to keep. I can't take Brad. Okay, kid? Huh? Just this once?" She started tickling me under my chin.

I ducked like a boxer and shook my head no while I said yes.

"Thanks, there's something in it for ya," she said, imitating a punch-drunk boxer and dancing around.

"Don't, Mom, it's okay. He still takes afternoon naps, doesn't he?"

She smiled brightly. "Sometimes."

Then she left. It took Malcolm five whole minutes to come back. When he did he was sitting on the lamp on my desk. Naturally, he fell right off onto the floor. There wasn't enough to sink into. But he didn't make any noise. Ghosts don't.

"Ugh, I have to baby-sit Brad on Saturday."

"Ah, yes, the little fellow," Malcolm said seriously.

"Brad never talks about you. But then again, he doesn't talk. He probably thinks you belong in the new house."

Malcolm giggled.

Then I continued my story. I told him how badly I felt when, in gym class, all the guys who play football in that field ignored me. If the gym teacher wasn't there I wouldn't have been on any of the soccer teams, either.

I turned away from Malcolm then. "I have a confession to make. I still sometimes go to the field on my bike and watch them play football. They play almost every day, only I've never been asked again. I sit there and pull clumps of grass out. I don't even think they know I'm there."

Malcolm cleared his throat. "Well, listen, Scottie. We can play football."

I spun around. "Two-hand touch?"

"Four-hand touch," he answered. "Anything's possible with me!"

Then we started to play and I knew what he meant. I taught him everything, and he was a fast learner. Our only problem, though we cleared some of the furniture away, was that he looked like an optical illusion because he was transparent. Sometimes he missed and the ball flew through him. Sometimes we ran into each other and he passed through me. But it sure was fun. And I fell asleep that night thinking that none of the guys who wouldn't let me play football had their very own ghost to play with. And I knew I had one real friend in the world. Or half in the world.

8
A Real Friend

On Friday afternoon, while I was sitting on the school bus, I couldn't help wishing that I had someone to talk to. I wouldn't have cared so much if the kids were just being rude. But they treated me as if I were invisible. That could give a guy the creeps.

I kept trying to start conversations with them. I would ask questions, such as, "Where's the pencil sharpener?" How many times can I ask that before they start to think I'm blind as well as deaf and mute? Or sometimes, just to hear myself talk out loud, I would ask, "What time is it?" Another one was, "Where's the water fountain?" I got an answer to each one, but no one really talked to me. As for the time, after a while they just pointed to the clock.

As I got off the bus I gave Tracy an especially mean, dirty look. She noticed it, too. I mean, where does it say that girls can't be nice to boys? She could have helped.

I slept late Saturday and then remembered Mom wanted me to baby-sit. Brad gets up early and messes around. I figured he'd be ready for an early nap, so as soon as my mom left I plunked him in the crib. He stood up, looked around, and climbed out.

"Look, Brad, don't give me any trouble."

". . . trouble," he said, jumping up and down.

"I don't care what you do. Sleep or not. But whatever you do, do it in your own room. I'll be right back."

Then I ran upstairs and got him two of my old comic books. When I returned he was still jumping up and down. He looked up at me happily and then sat on the floor shredding the comic books to bits. I thought that would do the trick. Comic books were a real treat for him.

Then I went through the house. Today it seemed bigger than most days. "Malcolm? Malcolm? Are you there? Can you materialize today?" Silence. Not even a shutter flapping or faint groaning sounds. Maybe he wasn't there at all.

I went into the guest bedroom where I had some model boats drying. I had put together the *Titanic* and the *Arizona,* and pretty soon I'll do a frigate. My dad is helping me. I really felt I had to stick to the same floor Brad was on. If I had gone to my room I wouldn't have been baby-sitting. And my mom was giving me a dollar an hour. From now on whenever I got stuck with him I would get paid.

On the top of the dresser there was a big mirror. Before I got to my boats I couldn't resist. First I started by doing my favorite faces. Then I invented new ones. I thought my faces were better than Ralphie's. *Gee,* I wonder what he's doing. I hadn't talked to him in about a week. I felt funny about calling him.

I pulled out the corners of my mouth. One eye was half open and the other was crossed. I heard a giggle.

And there in the mirror I saw first a head and then a torso slide under it and then the beginnings of legs and some arms. I turned around. By now I had seen Malcolm materialize in odd ways. But it never failed to astonish me.

"Hi, Malcolm, where've you been?"

"Oh, you know, my boy. My arthritis seems to come back when the leaves turn. Every fall for the last ninety-five years. I'm just not as quick as I used to be. What are these?"

"Model boats," I said. "I think they're all glued together and dry. Want to play?" Maybe it wouldn't be such a bad Saturday after all. Then I said, "Uh-oh."

We both turned. I had seen the top of his head through the mirror first. Just standing and staring. His thumb in his mouth.

"Cute little tyke, don't you think?" Malcolm said.

"No," I said right away.

"What's wrong, Brad. Did you rip all the comic books? I gave them to you so you would stay in your room."

Malcolm said, "I think you could let him stay."

"No, Malcolm, I wanted to play with you."

And then who should walk in but my mom. "Everything okay, darling?" she said.

I could feel my heart pumping. Maybe I'd faint. "Yeah, Mom. I thought you left."

"Oh, well, you know me. I needed gas and I didn't have my credit cards. Got to dash or I'm going to be late. How's everything? Who were you talking to, Scottie?"

"Hunh?"

"It sounded like you had a friend over."

"Uh-uh. I was just talking to Brad." We both looked over at Brad. He was still sucking his thumb. Then he took it out of his mouth and it made a snappy sound like something rubbery.

"Ghost," he said, nice and clear. I looked in the mirror out of the corner of my eye. I thought my face had turned snow-white.

"What's that, sweetheart?" Mom said, bending over until her head was almost level with his.

"Ghost!" he blasted. I thought she stumbled backward a little.

My mom looked at me angrily and pointed her finger. "Now, Scottie. You know I don't want you feeding him any of this ghost business. We don't believe in that kind of thing in this house. Besides I know what you've been doing. You're trying to spook him. And that's mean. He's only a baby."

I shook my head until it almost fell off. "No, Mom, honest. I don't know where he got *that* word. Maybe from TV. Gosh, I don't know why he even came in. I gave him my comic books to shred to keep him happy."

"Oh, that's nice, Scottie. I love it when you treat your younger brother nicely." Then, I don't know if it was my imagination, but it looked as if she was going to cry. "You're my oldest," she said, and ran out.

When she was gone and we heard the front door slam, Malcolm said, "Your mother is a definite nonbeliever."

"Oh, yeah. And my dad, too. They're into health food and yoga and all kinds of things. But no ghosts. I wonder how come I ended up in this family. But you know what they really bug me about?"

"What, Scottie?"

"The fact that they want me to have friends. I always had friends in my old neighborhood. My mom even got tired of them hanging around."

I turned and looked in the mirror. I was wearing jeans and a T-shirt that said The Cleveland Browns. I'm a little tall for my age, and no matter how much I eat, I just don't gain weight. I kind of live from meal to meal. My mom says one day it's going to catch up with me. I wish it would. I look like a sandy-haired string bean. In the beginning of the summer I'd gotten my hair cut too short, but it was starting to grow out.

"Malcolm, do I look like a creep?"

He looked puzzled.

"You know, a . . . loser. The kind of guy no one wants to be friends with."

"You look like a handsome, friendly lad to me, Scott boy."

"Because how can you be one of the guys in one place and then be totally ignored in another place? I'm not used to it."

"No one is. How do you think I feel? Talk about being ignored . . . !"

I laughed then. Sometimes Mr. Malcolm Mallory could make me laugh more than Ralphie used to. I looked at Brad. Suddenly I felt sorry for him. When he finally started to speak in real sentences, which he might do any day—at least we were all waiting—he would be on the outside immediately. Because he would want to share Malcolm. And no one would know what he was talking about. Except me, of course. And I wasn't going to make things easier for him.

"Maybe I should bring yuch-face Howard Fierman home and let him pick his nose and eat it in front of my mother. He'd pretend to be my friend."

"He'd probably like to be your friend. He's on the outside, too."

"Well, it's *his* fault."

"Did you *ever* tell him how bad it looks? Or . . . maybe the poor boy's hungry!"

Malcolm's belly shook. *"Blechhhh!"* I screamed and rolled on the floor laughing. *"Blechhhh!"* Brad screamed. Then he fell to his knees and rolled over and over on the carpet.

We laughed so hard tears were streaming down

my face but no sound was coming out of my mouth. Then we decided to go up to my room. I had to take Brad because I was baby-sitting him. But otherwise I would never let him in my room. As soon as he got in the door he started to run around and touch things.

"He's spoiled," I said to Malcolm.

"Sounds like you're a little jealous." Then he winked at me. "It could happen to Brad, too, you know."

"What?"

"A little brother or even sister."

"Nah." I shook my head. "My parents won't have any more kids. You know who I miss? I miss Ralphie. Gee, on Saturday, we would be going to the movies or playing two-hand touch. Ralphie and I were blood brothers, you know."

"Oh, really," Malcolm said.

"But now he's like a stranger. Not that much time has passed since I moved away. If I had stayed everything would be the same. We'd still be good friends."

"Of course. Friendships are like that. But it would have changed one day. You don't have to move in distance. And even if you move, sometimes you still stay friends. I have ghostly friends all over the world."

"Really?" I had never thought of other ghosts.

"Oh, of course. Sometimes when I disappear I'm off visiting a friend. We all have wonderful times. I have a friend who haunts a castle in England. He changes shapes and sizes at whim. You know, it takes me sometimes a day to assemble myself in that damp weather. We have some frightful times together."

"Wow, that would be fun to have a bunch of friends who are ghosts. Do you guys play games together, like football?"

"Well, no, we don't do that," he said. "And we're not all 'guys.' There are lady ghosts as well. And they're all my friends. They haunt big mansions and wrecked ships. Lovely creatures. I've always been faithful to my Martha, but they're still my friends. Some of them I met almost one hundred years ago, when I first started ghosting."

I listened to him. I knew my mouth was open.

"And that's my point, Scott," he went on. "It takes a while for a friendship to grow."

"But I haven't got a hundred years. I was hoping to make some friends before I went into sixth grade."

Malcolm laughed. "You will."

"Do you remember when you were a kid?" I asked him. "Didn't you have problems with friends?" Brad had conked out under the pinball machine, finally napping. Prince II was strangely quiet.

"Let's see. My youth. I remember it well. That was about one hundred and fifty years ago. Oh, we had different problems then. Not so many gadgets. And lots of brothers and sisters and cousins to play with. This whole area was farm land. I had lots of chores. But when we played we had fun. We'd go for a skinny-dip in the pond or have hayrides or go horseback riding through the woods."

"That sounds terrific—except for the horses. But how did you exist without color TV?"

"Oh, we managed. We talked to each other. And we played games. And told ghost stories." Then he got real serious. "We also didn't move around. I was born and raised in this neighborhood. That's your problem, isn't it, Scott? The fact that your folks moved."

"Yeah, it ruined my life. The only friend I have is you."

"Oh, you wait and see. You'll have friends. That's the nature of friendship. You outgrow friends you've had and you make new ones."

"Yeah, I outgrew Ralphie, that's for sure. And it happened so fast. He doesn't like me, either."

"Well, you live in this great big house. Maybe he feels funny around you."

"But that isn't being friends," I protested. "And we were supposed to be blood brothers."

Malcolm looked sad then. "No, it isn't real friendship. Real friends stay friends even if they're separated. The thing you want to remember is that you once were friends with Ralphie. And it was very real to you then. You should remember the good times, have no regrets, and go on to make other friends."

"But look at your ghost friends," I remembered. "You've been friends with them for a long, long time. You'll never part from them, you've known them so long."

"Well, someday I might have to leave them behind, my boy," he said mysteriously.

9

Silly Séance

Every day at school seemed the same. I was beginning to wonder if I would go all the way to the sev-
enth grade as an invisible person. Maybe Malcolm
was beginning to rub off on me. I was so nervous I
answered questions in class with this high-pitched
voice. It didn't even feel like it belonged to me. The
only time I really played with everyone was in gym.
They had to. No one ever used my name, though.
This was at least safe. But kids coming down the
steps would trip me if I tried to go up. The only reason I wasn't becoming the brunt of everyone's
meanness was that they already had someone.
Howard Fierman.

I tried to avoid him, but he sat next to me at
lunch. I'd try to look away and pretend he wasn't
there. But every once in awhile I got the urge to talk
to someone. Just to see if my voice worked between
eight and three. Actually, he wasn't stupid or anything. I could talk to him about my homework.

One time at lunch, though, I took a long look at

him and said, "Howard, take your finger out of your nose."

He looked up, startled. "What do you mean?"

"Your finger, your finger. Don't you know it's . . ." I couldn't continue. Obviously he didn't. It must have been a nervous habit.

He studied his finger. I folded up what was left of my peanut-butter-and-honey sandwich and threw it away. There was one little booger on the tip of his finger. Suddenly he saw it and brushed it away on the chair. He acted as though his finger was contaminated.

The days flew by. I was getting 100 percent on my math tests. I knew the teacher liked me. She probably felt sorry for me. And the last thing I needed was to be known as a goody-goody. The thing was, nobody let me be me. It's awfully hard to show any personality when you're not even talking.

The only place I felt comfortable was at home. And that was about over, because the first Parents-Teachers Night was in October. Then the truth would come out. Mrs. Simon would probably tell my parents I had a social problem. Then they would have to get me a psychologist.

I was still making up stories to tell my parents. I wanted them to think I was a normal ten-year-old kid, who would be eleven in November. It was just that I lived too far away from the rest of the kids for them to come over. Sometimes I pretended to call somebody. Good thing they never listened in on the other end. There was always a dial tone.

I sensed there was something strange going on between my parents. They didn't have to tell me. I knew they had a secret by the way they acted. They were doing that mushy Jack-and-Jill stuff again. Especially at the table.

"You look absolutely radiant, Jill."

"Oh, do you think so, Jack?"

And on and on it went. It's a wonder I didn't lose a pound a day with yuch-face Fierman at lunch and my parents doing that stuff at the dinner table.

I always told them about the same thing.

Them: And how was your day, Scott?

Me: Fine. I got another hundred on my math test.

Them: Maybe you'll be a mathematician, or an engineer.

Me: You know I want to be a football player.

Them: What did you do after school?

Me: You know, I played football with the guys. Mikey and the gang.

Mom: Listen, Scott, if your friends live that far away I'll be glad to pick them up and take them home again.

Me: No, that's okay, Mom. I see them in school and at the yard. They live really far away. Chagrin Falls is a big place.

Mom again: But how come you never go to birthday parties like you used to?

Me: Aw, gee, Mom. I'm a year older practically. They don't have birthday parties anymore. A few of the kids are starting to date.

I figured that was pushing it. But I was running out of answers. I buried everything by keeping my mouth full of food. I would eat two desserts sometimes. That's one of the great things about being skinny. I burn it up real fast. Plus, I'm always hungry when I'm unhappy.

After dinner I usually went to my room to play. Malcolm was always right behind me, or sometimes he passed me and crossed through me. Then he was right in front of me. I never knew what he was going to do. Every once in awhile he would do something outrageous. It would crack me up.

Like the night I was lying on the hooked rug watching TV in the family room. I looked up, and marching past the window was Malcolm holding a pumpkin on his head. It really took me by surprise. I rolled on the floor laughing. One problem. The program we were watching was about hopelessly poor, undernourished children in the third world.

I looked up and saw my parents gaping at me. Boy, was that embarrassing.

Then there was the time Malcolm and I decided to play ball outside. It was just a simple catch game with a softball. I didn't know my mom was outside. I thought she was in the basement working. How could I know she was coming toward us? There I was, throwing a ball and it was coming back to me, a boomerang. Fortunately, Malcolm warned me. We were playing near the woods as we always do. Quickly I maneuvered myself against the back part of the house closer to the front. When she came up all she said was, "Scottie, I really wish you wouldn't play ball against the house. Daddy put up a basketball net for you."

When she left, Malcolm and I couldn't stop laughing. Sometimes Malcolm did some spooky things without even trying. Tonight we were playing two-hand touch in my room. The game got fast and furious. I picked up the football and ran to the pinball machine before I realized I was holding Malcolm's head in my hands. I screamed and then dropped his head. Then I put my hands over my mouth. What if someone heard me?

Malcolm's head rolled across the floor toward him. He put it back on and said, "I'm really not myself. It's time for me to leave here, Scottie, my boy."

I was stunned—like someone had punched me in the stomach. I couldn't speak for a minute. "Leave. You just got here! Besides, where would you go? Not everyone can see you, you know. I mean, it's not that easy to leave if no one knows you've been here."

Malcolm put up his hand to stop me. It immediately fell off.

"See," he smiled sheepishly. "I think it's a sign from . . . Martha."

"Your . . ."

"Yes, my wife, my dearly departed Martha, who left this earthly world at a ripe old age and is calmly resting on the Other Side. Which is where I'd rather be. If the powers that be deem it in their power to let me be there."

I guess I must have really looked sad then, because he said, "Now, look, Scott. It's just a plan. I'm not going anywhere. I know you need a friend, and I won't let you down. Besides, I can't go anywhere yet. I don't know how. We need to talk to Martha."

"How?" I asked, fascinated.

"Oh, a séance, of course."

"But don't you need living people—no offense—to do that sort of thing?"

"We have you. This is a ghost séance so there's quite a difference. I shall call upon my medium, Napatha, a ghost nearby. She contacted Martha about ten years ago. Ghosts have no sense of time. Seems like an hour ago."

"Where should we set up?" I asked, feeling excited.

"We need a table . . ."

"My desk," I replied.

"Fine, Scottie. And one dim lamp . . ."

"My clown lamp," I suggested.

"Excellent. We need some candles . . ."

"Here." I reached in my drawer and found some skinny birthday candles. Then I dashed downstairs and got some soft, cakelike cookies. They would work as candleholders. With my appetite, my mom wouldn't even question missing cookies. I put them all around my room and punched a hole for the little candles.

"A tablecloth . . ."

"My bedspread," I almost shouted.

"Perfect," Malcolm said. "We're ready to begin." I felt a chill.

Prince II slunk through the door to take his place behind my chair. I patted his head. "Nice dog, good boy," I murmured.

Malcolm explained the séance. It would be like trying to telephone Martha long distance and using Napatha as the long-distance operator.

We touched fingertips. Then Malcolm chanted in a funny voice. "Spirit world, throw from your midst, Napatha." He said that about twenty-five times. I was beginning to think they didn't want to let her go. Then, suddenly, there was this wavy, bubbly voice that was very faint and didn't at all sound human. It sounded like an underwater fish.

The voice said, or burbled, "Do you have to bother me, Mal, while I'm having the swim of my life."

Malcolm's stomach shook the way it did when he laughed. "Where in heaven are you, Nappy?"

"My dear," came the sparkling bubble sound. "I'm having a swim. At the Taj Mahal. Such a lovely night, Mal. You really should do it sometime."

"Very romantic," Malcolm said. Then he whispered, chuckling, "She's not alone you know."

Just then we heard a crack of lightning, and I

looked outside. It wasn't raining. The sound swelled and got thinner. It was the longest crack of lightning I ever heard—sort of like a beam of sound.

"Love her laugh," Malcolm said to me. Then he looked out the window and shut his eyes. "Napatha, I want to talk to Martha."

Again the silvery voice. Every letter seemed to shimmer. It was higher, though, and sounded more like a girl's than a woman's. "Your dearly departed," the voice sang sweetly.

"My dearly departed," Malcolm repeated. I looked at him then. He didn't seem to be the Malcolm I played with. He just sat like a sad, old man. He reminded me of my grandpa when my grandma Lil had to have her gallbladder taken out.

"Ready?" the wavy voice said. Then the table began to rise and rock as if it were a ship in the water. I gulped. I tried to tell myself it was a prank, but I was scared. I mean, a ghost was one thing but a whole network of ghosts! And Napatha frightened me. She was like one of those ghosts that Malcolm had told me about. The ones that change shape and personality. I wondered if she really was a fish that night. Or half-fish, half-lady or something from outer space.

Out of nowhere, a cat landed on the windowsill. I gasped. How did it get there? None of the trees outside were high enough to leap from. The cat jumped to the top of my bookcase and leaped down onto the middle of the table. It hissed at us, and I shivered. Then, while I watched in astonishment, the cat jumped off the table and . . . vanished. Just disappeared. I almost fell through the floor. I thought I'd have a nervous breakdown. Malcolm didn't seem to notice. He kept his eyes closed.

"Napatha, you're not concentrating. It's Martha I want." I stared up at him, wide-eyed. He opened one eye and winked. "She dabbles in reincarnation a lot. Sometimes she sends the wrong ones."

"Martha, Martha," he mumbled intensely.

I wanted to help him. "Martha, Martha," I said softly over and over. I wondered if she would show up in person. Would she look like a nice little old, real old, lady or would she clink through the door like a skeleton?

There was a sound. A dragging footstep. I shivered and prayed I wouldn't faint. I made sure my eyes were squeezed shut.

"Martha," Malcolm whispered. "You're here at last." His voice sounded happier than I had heard it in a long time.

There was silence. Time seemed to stand still. And then it was broken. With a big, long burp. My eyes flew open. Malcolm and I spun around in our chairs. And there in the corner stood . . . Brad. He was wearing his old sleeper pajamas, the ones that used to cover his feet before he grew out of them and my mom cut off the feet. He was dragging his raggedy blanket.

He ruined the whole thing! The spell was broken. Now, Martha would never show up.

"What are you doing here?" I shouted at him, furiously.

Brad just stood there for a moment, sucking his thumb and clutching his blanket. Then he left the room. "He knows he's not allowed in my room," I said to Malcolm.

"Maybe there's a reason for it," Malcolm said mysteriously. "Maybe Martha and I aren't destined to be together just yet."

I felt bad for him, but in a way I was glad. He was my only friend. Who would I have if he went away? We played pinball until I had to go to bed. I couldn't imagine life without Malcolm. I just couldn't.

10
The Mummy's Case

Funny how your life can change when you least expect it to—almost overnight. When it happened I was sure Malcolm had something to do with it. I couldn't wait to thank him. And I couldn't wait to begin our séance again. It was better than any of the thriller pictures my mom and dad let me see.

But I couldn't find Malcolm. I walked around for an hour outside, muttering softly, "Malcolm, Malcolm." Then I tried it for another half-hour in my room. I began to get a little angry. He was still playing tricks. Just like Ralphie. Why did I think of Ralphie just then? Now it was as if he'd never existed. But I guess it was because it was getting nearer to Halloween. It was the first time in my life I would be going trick-or-treating without him.

I happened to look out the window, and I did a double take. I was looking at the top of Malcolm's head. He was sitting in the tree below me, looking rumpled and scratching his head. He seemed to have just waked up.

"Malcolm," I called down, "what are you doing sitting in that tree?"

He looked around and started talking to a robin that had perched on a nearby branch.

"Malcolm," I yelled. "Why don't you come up here? What's wrong? It's me, Scottie." I was beginning to get a little worried.

Then he recognized me.

At the same time, I felt as though someone was standing in the doorway. It was my mom. Her hands were on her hips.

"Scottie, what's all the shouting about? Who *is* up here?"

After awhile this kind of thing can get on a guy's nerves. And after awhile it's not funny. It's not my fault if she doesn't believe. I looked down at the tree. Malcolm had vanished.

Keeping my eyes down, I said with a straight face, "I'm practicing a speech for school. That's all, Mom." Then I added for effect, "You didn't hear another voice, did you?"

"No, that's right, I didn't," she said, as if I had been trying to trick her. "What's your speech on? I'd love to hear you do it, Scottie. You know I was a drama major in college. We should sit down and talk. It's been a long time since we did that. I didn't mean to interrupt your privacy, it's just that . . ."

"Not now, Mom," I said, cutting her off. I knew I was being slightly rude, but I just had to talk to Malcolm. "Listen, maybe later, huh? See, I have this

speech and then I have my math problems and then
. . . I might play football with the guys later."

She looked at me. I sensed she didn't believe
me. I think she'd stopped buying the idea that I had
friends and just thought I was odd. At Parents-
Teachers Night it had been so crowded all Mrs. Simon could tell my parents was that I was her best
math student. Then Mrs. Simon got stuck serving re-
freshments, and they couldn't talk to her. My mom
said she'd call for an appointment to talk to her
alone. So far she hadn't done it.

Malcolm materialized on top of the pinball machine. I couldn't help but laugh. He ran to the door
and jumped in front of my mom as she was leaving.
Then he stepped aside and bowed. My mom walked
right through him, anyway.

"Guess what!" I said, not wanting to wait any
longer. I was almost exploding with excitement.

But he interrupted me. "Sorry I'm late, but
there was an earthquake on Venus." He threw his
hands up in desperation.

"How do you know?"

"Light signals from an old friend who just took
off one day for Venus."

"You mean there are ghosts on . . . other planets?"

He smiled. "Of course. We're not limited to
spaceships or other conventional forms of space
transportation. I can get to Venus or Mars and back
in no time at all."

"But do they look like we do? People on other planets?"

"Oh, I don't know anything about the people. You see, ghosts can't see people on other planets. Only other ghosts. But people on other planets can supposedly see ghosts. I'll tell you, the ghosts are ghastly."

"Wow!" Malcolm was so fascinating. I almost forgot what I had to tell him.

"Wait a second!" I screamed. "I have some news! Guess what?"

"I give," he said, shrugging.

Funny thing about Malcolm. He was beginning to sound more like a ten-year-old kid every day.

I stared him down. "Still give?"

He nodded, and I noticed his head was kind of wobbly. I was thankful when he stopped. Malcolm had so much energy. He didn't know when to slow down. That's why he was always leaving something behind lately. A hand, a foot, an arm.

"Well, okay, but I think you already know. Because you probably had something to do with it."

I studied his face very carefully. He just looked interested. It was probably a trick.

"Our class went on a field trip today. To the Cleveland Art Museum. It's really pretty. I saw it once before. They have this lagoon in front with swans, and we got to feed them."

Malcolm said, "Oh, I know. I wish they'd take those swans out. I like to swim there, but it's just so messy. All those bread crumbs people throw in the lake." He chuckled. "Not the same kind of class as Nappy with her Taj Mahal dips."

I was impatient to get to the heart of my story. "Okay, we ate our box lunches there. Anyway, we get in the museum, and we go through all these rooms. Most have paintings but some have furniture roped off. It's okay, except there's this musty smell. Then we get to the Egyptian room and the mummies." I couldn't help starting to giggle. "Tracy and her girlfriends are in one group. Mikey and his gang are in another. These two other girls, Sheila and Suzanne, are lagging behind. Me and Howard Fierman are right up front.

"Just then we come to this huge thing. It looks like a curved wardrobe closet, but it's a mummy case. And the teacher says the mummy is inside, fully preserved and wrapped over and over."

Malcolm nodded.

"Mikey is going to the back of the case as the whole class moves on. He says, '*Hooooooo*, the ghost of the mummy is in the case, and I'm going to let it out.' A few of his buddies are watching, deciding whether to stay and get in trouble or go with the teacher. They leave. But I thought you might do something, so I stayed. Mikey sticks his hand underneath the rim of the mummy's case, and he gets three fingers caught in it!

"The class is going toward the medieval section and no one really misses us yet. See, there's a quiz on the museum when we get back. Meanwhile

Mikey can't get his fingers out. He's tugging and pulling but they're stuck in a mummy's case that's thousands of years old. I think he thought that a ghost had grabbed him, because his face turned red. He was scared. Then he panicked because he couldn't get his fingers out. Big Mikey started to cry.

"I just stared. Big Mikey crying. He looked at me. I looked at him. I mean, here was a kid who made my life really miserable. I could have just walked away and left him there crying."

"What did you do?" Malcolm asked.

"Well, I went to get Mr. Macri, the teacher who took us on the field trip. And you know what?"

"What?" he said.

"Before I left, Mikey said, 'Wait a minute, Scottie.' He called me by my name. I couldn't believe it. 'You know my name?' I said. His face was really white. I thought he would pass out. Then he said, 'The ghost has caught me by my fingers. Promise me one thing?' I wanted to tell him I knew the ghost, but I didn't. I just said, 'What?' He said, 'Promise me you won't tell the other guys you saw me cry.'

"I looked at him and nodded. Then I ran to get the teacher. Mr. Macri had to get a guard, and they had to call an ambulance to take Mikey to the hospital."

"Oh, dear me, I hope he was all right."

I looked at Malcolm oddly. "Of course. He came back to school that afternoon to show everyone his hand. His three middle fingers looked just like a mummy's hand. They were wrapped in big bandages. He also bragged a lot. He scared the girls, telling them there was a ghost in the mummy's case. But he talked to me after school. And after that the other guys talked to me, too. And even Tracy smiled at me. Mikey asked me for my phone number. So, I just want to say thank you."

Malcolm was smiling. "Thanks for what, Scott?"

"You know. Being the ghost that grabbed Mikey's fingers inside the mummy's case so it could all happen."

Malcolm shook his head. "No, Scott. I wasn't the ghost in the mummy's case. Don't know who it might have been. Before my time, you know."

"It wasn't you?" I couldn't believe it.

"No, Scott. I wasn't on the trip with you. You did it. You saw he was in trouble, and you wanted to help him. You weren't spiteful and offered your friendship. Though he had held his back. You were honorable and didn't snitch on him."

I was shocked. "No trick, Malcolm?"

"No. In fact, you know where I was today? All day long I was trying to materialize. The wind was blowing in my direction. The sun was shining. Twice, I ended up on the tops of telephone poles. Once, in the duck pond, with everything on backward. You saw how hard it was trying to come in here. Missed by a wide margin. Ever see me up a tree, like that?"

"Come to think of it, no," I answered. "Hey, maybe you have a cold. It's going around now."

"No cold. Just old. I was never cut out for

ghosting. It was just thrust on me. No how-to-haunt books, no oil-your-chains-the-easy-way booklets. No voice training for the correct, scary moan or scream. Oh, no, I had to learn the hard way. I'm self-taught you know."

"Gosh," I said. "You really sound depressed."

I heard a mournful doggy sob from underneath the bed. Prince II stuck his head out and then retreated back under.

"And this century." He sat down on my bed and sighed. "No one believes in me."

"*I* believe in you!" I protested. "And I don't know if Brad does, but he must. He sees you."

"I know. But if people saw me on that little box you call television, they wouldn't believe in me."

I'd never heard Malcolm talk that way before.

"And the noise," he continued. "When I was living here, and even when haunting was a bit of a treat, you could smell the grass and hear the chickens and the horses and the birds. Now all you hear are horseless carriages!"

"It's not so bad here, Malcolm. Really. This is the country. You should try living in the city. Hey," I said quickly, trying to snap him out of it. "Why don't we try to contact Martha again. Maybe this time we'll reach her. That should make you feel better."

"We talked today," he said flatly.

"What! You had a séance without me. Gee, Mal, you could have waited until I got home from school."

Napatha had some spare time. Besides, it
t a real séance, Scott. Martha came to me in a
vision."

"Wow, what kind of a vision?"

"Well, she was wearing one of her black silk
dresses with a lace collar and a cameo brooch. Martha never changes." Then his voice became low and
mysterious, "Also, Scottie, they don't often allow
people from the Other Side over. She was carrying a
message."

"Wow, what was the message?"

"She said just one thing to me, and then she
disappeared. *Poof!* Just like that. I can still see her
now, with her elegant gray hair swept up on the top
of her head in a knot. Her glittering gray eyes. And
her wrinkled peaches-and-cream complexion."

"What did she say?"

He looked wistful then. "She said, 'What are
you still hanging around for, dummy?' "

Malcolm looked sad. "I wish she could have
stayed longer," he said. "But the point is, Scott boy,
I'm pooped. You have new friends now. It's time for
me to cross over to the Other Side where I belong."

"Then you did everything on purpose," I insisted.

"What? Hold that insensitive boy's precious fingers in a mummy's case? Not for a minute, Scottie.
Don't you believe it. You won his friendship all by
yourself. By the way, whatever will become of
Howard, the boy with the . . . er . . . problem?"

"I didn't sit with him on the bus today. I sat with the other guys."

"Ah. So he remains on the outside. Alone."

"Don't say it so . . . so dramatically! It's his own fault. He's yuchhy."

"Yes," Malcolm said with a smile. "So yuchhy he was willing to be your friend when no one else was. And now, when you desert him, he probably won't say anything."

I saw what he meant. Malcolm had a way of making things clear. "Yeah, but Howard? That would mean I would have to make him accepted. That's impossible. How can I do that?"

"You'll figure it out," Malcolm said. He could also be maddening.

"No, you! You're the one who's good at figuring out everything!"

"Now there's where you're wrong, my boy. For example, I can't figure out how to leave. Can you help me?"

I looked at him, astonished. He was really serious. How could I help him? I didn't want him to leave. He was my best friend.

11
Giving Up the Ghost

I felt sad. I looked at Malcolm. He seemed a lot worse. I don't think he could have played a practical joke on me if his life depended on it. It was hard to understand his predicament, not being a ghost. I just knew I had to help him, because he had helped me so much. Even if it meant I had to lose him.

"Malcolm?" I asked. "You keep saying you had an untimely death, and that's how you became a ghost. What happened?"

"Ah, yes," he sighed. "That's a perfect place to begin, Scottie. At the beginning. I wasn't yet fifty when it happened. There was a windmill." He went to my window and pointed. "See out there near the driveway to the next house? Toward the stables?" I squinted and tried to imagine a big windmill near the woods. Though I thought they only had them in Holland.

"We used it for pumping water," Malcolm added. "One windy day I was up inside making some needed repairs. Martha had packed me a lunch, in a basket. I shall never forget it. Half a roast chicken, her delicious corn bread, a container of bean salad, a jar of lemonade." I looked at the size of Malcolm's waistline and understood. "And a banana," he continued. "Ah, yes, the fatal banana.

"I finished my lunch and tossed the banana peel in the basket. But alas, I missed. When I was done with my work, I went back to get the basket. I skidded on the banana peel all the way across the floor, fell out the window, and landed on the sails of the windmill, which were going around ferociously in a strong gust of wind. Then I fell to the ground . . . in parts. That's why I have trouble materializing when the wind isn't right."

I sat there staring at him, my mouth wide open. Then I reached up and closed my mouth.

"It was untimely," I said. "And weird, too."

"That's why I got to be a ghost."

"You know, maybe you could sell that story to the movies. They love stories full of blood."

"Oh, it was all very painless for me, really. It was harder on Martha. Poor woman. She had to go looking for me. No easy job. But I got to linger. It's just becoming too much for me, you see. I'm a tired, old ghost."

"And you want to cross over to the Other Side," I said.

He nodded so energetically that I felt myself getting ready to catch his head in case it dropped off.

I knew I had to help him. But how? Boy, I've

thought about a lot of things in my day. What costume to wear for Halloween. How to make creamy
peanut butter interesting. But this?

As I thought, I paced around. Then I raised my
hand. It was automatic.

"I've got it!" I shouted.

Malcolm perked up. "Look, you can go to
Venus or Mars or anywhere. Why not just materialize
on the Other Side."

"Because," he said sadly. "It's on the Other
Side. It's a little harder to find. I know where the
planets are. But I've never been to the Other Side."

I felt stupid. I paced some more. Malcolm
paced. I walked through him accidentally and apolo-
gized. Then we paced farther apart. Prince II was
following me, turning as I turned, a hangdog expres-
sion on his face.

Then I turned too sharply. I stumbled over
Prince II, bumped into the pinball machine, and
passed through Malcolm.

"I know!" I said, snapping my fingers.

"Yes?"

"Bring Martha back and tell her you're ready to
go with her."

He looked out the window when he answered. I
got the shivers. "That wasn't Martha I spoke to."

"But you said . . ."

"No, Scottie, it was merely a vision. As if it were
telegraphed by the mind. She couldn't come to fetch
me even if she wanted to. Besides, Martha was never
much for traveling."

We sat around. Neither of us spoke. We just concentrated. Then an idea crept into my mind. I was afraid to say it because the other ones had been so bad. But the thing is, with a real friend you're comfortable to say stupid things.

"Malcolm, did you ever hear of reenacting the scene of the crime?"

He scrunched up his forehead. "Detective stories, hmmmm? Sherlock Holmes and all that?"

I held my breath.

"Well, it's worth a try."

"Yes?" I said, jumping up.

"Absolutely. My unfortunate accident happened before sunset. I know because I was looking forward to dinner." Then he winced. "What's today's date, my boy?"

"October twenty-fifth."

"It was in May when it happened. May twenty-fifth, actually."

"What was the weather like?"

"Oh, it was a cold day in May."

"Funny, but it's a mild day in October. Look at the leaves rolling across the lawn. The trees are bending with the wind. Looks as if a storm's coming."

"It's a terrible idea!" Malcolm shouted then. "Let's try it!" We marched out of my room. Prince II followed us, but didn't come outside.

I had a quirky feeling throughout all of this. Especially when I spotted my mother watching me march out of the house.

Malcolm twirled one way. And then he whirled the other way. "The windmill was right about here, I think," he said. "Shame they tore it down. So scenic. Now what do we do, Scott, my boy?"

That was a good question. We had figured out the setting for the crime. "Concentrate," I said loudly. It was almost as if someone had put the idea into my head. "Keep thinking of where you want to go. Did you ever wish on a star?"

"Oh, several times. Sometimes I was sitting right on it."

"Okay then, shut your eyes. Now think of Martha. And think of how much you want to join her. Picture going to the Other Side. Maybe someone will help you if you concentrate hard enough."

We were very still then. Like people are when they're praying.

Usually I just feel one feeling. I'm happy. Or I'm sad. Or I'm angry. But for the first time in my life, while we were standing there, I felt lots of things at the same time. I was happy for Malcolm because I cared about him. I was unhappy for me because if this worked I sure would miss him. I was angry at Martha because—why did he have to like a girl better than me? We could have played together at least until I was twenty.

Well, maybe not, because I would be a teenager first. Maybe I wouldn't have any time to be with Malcolm. I would probably be playing on the football team or maybe I would want to be with girls. Actually that might not be as dopey as I originally thought. Tracy Deevers cut off those rope braids and her hair curls around her face. I keep looking at her. And she keeps looking back at me. Still, I know she's stupid. But in my teen-age years I knew I would change somehow. Maybe I'd be a teen-ager when I turned twelve, or even eleven. A lot of girls in our school were.

I was so busy thinking about myself I didn't notice that Malcolm wasn't there. I guess I expected a puff of smoke or something where he had been standing. On the other hand, just because I didn't see him didn't mean he had actually gone. He might materialize in the duck pond.

I looked around. Everything felt odd. I seemed to be standing in a pool of quiet. A private circle. Something was missing. Suddenly I felt sad. All the other feelings were gone. I'd just lost my best friend. I was hoping against hope he hadn't made it to the Other Side.

I looked toward the horizon. The sun was sinking like a big red ball. It was glowing hot pink against the blue. Funny, I hadn't noticed things like that much before.

I kept looking around. I saw the window in our huge kitchen, which faced the back woods. Then I saw my mom looking out. She was eyeing me curiously. I must have looked dumb. Standing there, listening, waiting, probably looking sad, as if I was going to cry.

Again I had to cover up for Malcolm. I ran in the back door and began to pretend I was reciting my so-called speech for school. I just made it up as I went along.

Pointing my finger into the air, I shouted, "Whence does he go?"

Then I skipped back a few steps pretending I had a sword in my hand. "He goes to the Other Side. Whence . . ." My mom interrupted me with applause. It was kind of good. Whatever I was saying. "Oh, very good, Scottie!" she said. "And very dramatic. Is that what you were doing standing in the woods walking around and talking?"

I took a deep breath. "Yep. Practicing my speech. But silently. You don't have to do it out loud."

"Oh, I know. Maybe you'll be a politician or a trial lawyer or sell things on television."

I wanted to be alone in the worst way. I knew Malcolm was gone for good. But I had to check. The sadness was going, and I began to feel happy for him. He really was a good friend. I had to find out if he'd made it. But I wasn't sure how I could really know.

"Sit down, Scott," Mom said. She poured me a glass of milk and put out some wheat-germ cookies. "I have something to tell you."

I looked at the counter. I remembered when I had seen Malcolm at the beginning. He was sitting there with his big belly, swinging his legs, putting down the banana peel. I had to cover for him. I guess I must have been smiling a little, then.

My mom said, "Oh, you know already, don't you?"

"No. Know what?"

"You know."

"No, honestly, Mom. I don't."

"Okay, have it your way. I'm going to have a baby."

"Oh, is that it? Gee, I thought you had put on some weight," I said.

"You don't mind, do you, Scott?"

"No, another little brother. What the heck. I can handle that." Two Brads. Great.

"And what if it's a little girl?" She was smiling.

"Oh, well. They're okay, too, I guess."

My mom picked up a cookie and crunched into it. "It's Brad I'm worried about. He'll be the middle child. Plus he'll go through what you went through. Having to play second fiddle to a baby."

I smiled real wide then. "Yeah, I guess he will."

Just then we saw Brad. He was looking under a chair. Then he hopped up, stood on tiptoe, and looked in a drawer. He looked as though he was going to cry. My mom snatched him up and put him on her lap. That was when I knew. Brad knew, too. Malcolm had really gone.

"Ghost," he said.

"Too much television," Mom said, clucking her tongue to the roof of her mouth.

"Excuse me, Mom," I said, in a hurry. "I have some homework to do before dinner." I raced up to my room. It was almost too much for one day. Another brother. Or a sister? Or what if it were twins? I could spend half my life baby-sitting.

But more important—Malcolm. It seemed as if I knew him all my life, but actually it wasn't even two months. He had taught me a lot of things about friendship. What it's like to be a real friend. About growing up and changing. Changing can be painful while you're going through it. But when you finish you feel much better about yourself.

I thought about Howard Fierman. How could I help him? I couldn't let him be the only outsider. He might be all mixed up when he got to be a teen-ager. He might go out and shoot someone or steal cars. Maybe I could have a birthday party. I'd invite him and that would start him being included. But mostly I had to tell him to stop picking his nose.

I was sitting on my bed, looking out the window, and I saw a big cloud rolling past. There was something strange about that cloud. It was in the shape of a jolly, fat man with a big belly. A hand was waving. I was stunned. Was it my imagination?

The window was open. I heard a whisper drift in on the wind. It was almost like the tinkling of bells.

"Goodbye, my friend."

So faint. But it was unmistakably Malcolm's voice. I spun around. Maybe it was coming from the room and he hadn't gone at all. Then I turned to look at the clouds. The strange cloud wasn't there, or had blended in with the others. But I knew I had seen him wave goodbye. I knew he had gone to the Other Side.

Prince II ran around the room, chasing his tail and yipping merrily. I guess he never felt too comfortable with a ghost in the house.

Then I heard my mom's voice calling from the middle of the second-floor landing. She sounded as if she was trying not to be excited.

She hollered, "Scott! Phone call for you! It's Mike."

ABOUT THE AUTHOR

Around the age of ten JUDI MILLER stumbled upon her first haunted house, in a blackberry patch, in Madison, Ohio. Ever since, she has been fascinated with spooky things and writes suspense thrillers for adults. Two of her mysteries are *Save the Last Dance for Me* and *I'll Be Wearing a White Carnation*. She also is a tap dancer, plays the piano, acts and sings, and is terribly afraid of ghosts.